SLIPPERY WHEN WET

WATCHERS CREW BOOK 4

INES JOHNSON

THOSE JOHNSON GIRLS

ONE

"Nurse Cleo, just what do you think you're doing?"

Dr. West's voice was shrill, like a varsity quarterback being stripped naked by the president of the geek club, then jeered at by the JV chess club, mocked by the extras in the theater club, and pointed at by the full cheer squad.

"I came in for a prostate exam," he said.

"Hmm," I purred, picking up the speculum and advancing towards him.

He lay back with his feet in stirrups, his knees up on an exam table. His bare ass cheeks clenched on my approach. My lips curled like a cat approaching a bowl of cream.

"So why are you giving me an anal exam?" he demanded.

I pulled on latex gloves, stretching the synthetic material down my fingers and then letting go of the end with a satisfying snap. West winced and my tummy tightened in anticipation. There was nothing in the world like watching a powerful man squirm as you slow marched toward him. Like a secretary who was smarter than her boss; like a wife who doctored the joint bank account; like a little girl wrapping her daddy around her pinky finger.

Dr. Simon West was the current big man on campus here at Sacred Heart Hospital. He had a string of letters after his name and a stack of medical journal articles by and about him. Everyone, including the Chief of Surgery, cowered in his wake.

Not me.

The bigger and louder they were, the wetter my panties got to bend them to their knees. In Dr. West's case, his knees were already bent. Bent back towards his belly with his ass presented in offering.

"I demand you let me up now, nurse." He spat the word *nurse* like it was an insult.

I gave his knees a shove, and they spread wider without protest. The speculum slid easily into his ass. He tried to squirm away, but he didn't get far. He opened his mouth in what looked like an attempt at a scream, but it turned into a moan.

He liked it.

That wouldn't do. I cranked the device open. It turned the small opening of his anus into a large hole.

"Awww!"

There was the music my ears were waiting for.

"Dr. West," I said. "I'm checking your exit because you seem to have a problem putting your penis inside too many entrances."

West raised his ass as I gave the speculum one more crank. His erect penis lay shackled at his belly. The eye of his penis wept. The twin baby blues on his face watered as well.

"It's as I expected," I tsked. "These tests show that you suffer from chronic masturbation."

He squirmed on the exam table. In the stirrups used to examine women's cervixes, all ten of West's toes arched back towards his body. His ass was scooted down to the edge of the table. His thighs spread wide like a woman having her yearly pap.

"There's only one cure; we need to plug this hole." I gave the speculum in his ass another crank.

He gripped the table. His knuckles went white. His eyes glazed over in pleasure.

"There's nothing wrong with me." His voice was

breathless, his chest heaved. "I demand you stop this now."

"I'm only trying to help you," I said.

"You're just a nurse," he panted. "You don't know what you're doing."

I snorted. "You surgeons all think you're God. The truth is that I save more lives in a week than you will ever save in your entire career. Whereas you couldn't find the scalpel without a nurse standing next to you. Isn't that right?"

I yanked the speculum from his hungry ass. He wailed in protest. His penis jerked inside its cage.

"What was that?" I said.

"Yes, Nurse Cleo." His blue eyes were glassy as he turned over his power to me.

The crotch of my blue scrubs went damp at the wild look in his eyes. It was a look of complete submission. My grin spread on the right side of my mouth, stretching East at the wickedness of it all. Now that I had his full attention, we could begin.

I cupped his balls in one hand and reached for the dildo with the other. Dr. West may have been a lion in the halls of the hospital, but I was about to turn him into a pussycat.

I held up the monster dick for him to see. His eyes widened, and he gulped. I wondered if he actually wanted me to do this? Not that it mattered. He was the type that would never safe word. He saw it as a sign of weakness. He was lucky I was a compassionate sadist.

I liked to make my subs suffer. But I also liked to play with them again and again. So, I tried not to break them. At least not irreparably. I oiled up the monster dick as Sacred Heart Hospital's heterosexual god panted in anticipation.

At some point in their lives, every man wants to be pegged. They're men, after all. They walk the earth pretending they have all the answers. But deep down inside, they're all little boys afraid of the awesome power that they wield between their legs.

It was a fantasy; a man that was actually in charge. Men could pretend all they wanted that they ruled the world. Most men walked a straight line. It was women that turned. Just like a boss, or a husband, or a clueless father, they all needed a woman's touch. It just so happened that I liked touching men's asses.

"Please," he whispered. "No."

West shook his head left to right. His thighs fell farther open as he held onto the idea that I was forcing him into this lewd act. As if I could force this six foot, two hundred twenty pound, testosterone-riddled man into anything. Not with all five foot four and one hundred sixty pounds of me.

Physically, I may have been your average woman. But my sexual proclivities were entirely, and wholly, and completely deviant. I shoved a bottle of lube up West's ass. His entire body shook and trembled at the invasion.

"Please hold your composure, Dr. West." I lined up the dildo with his hungry hole. "This is a necessary medical procedure. It should not arouse you."

As the dildo breached the first layer of his anus, he didn't tense. He completely relaxed under the assault. His eyes closed, and he had the look of a sub who was lost in a storm of pleasure.

The drip in my panties stopped. I knew I should have brought the thicker dildo. I'd already pegged him three times this week, and he'd adjusted. The good doctor was like an addict who'd tried weed on Monday and graduated to coke by Thursday.

I withdrew the fake dick. His eyes flew open like a newborn who'd heard a loud noise. His mouth formed a pouty O like he was about to let out a wailing cry. "What the fuck, Cleo?"

"What did you just call me?" I flicked at the pink cock cage that held his erection. His penis strained inside the metal bars.

"I mean, Mistress."

"Don't call me that either." I slapped his balls and his ass arched off the table. "You wish I was your Mistress. That's something you have to earn and you're not worthy. It's Nurse Cleo to you."

West's eyes were dilated. He was almost too far gone; lost in pleasure when I'd only given pain and frustration. Getting him off was too easy. I was getting bored.

Time to make this interesting. I slipped off my bottom scrubs and thong. West's eyes latched onto the key that dangled from my earlobe. It matched the lock to the cock ring he'd been wearing all day. I flicked my hair over my shoulder until it covered the ring. Some of the excitement left West's eyes.

I grinned as I climbed aboard the exam table. I hovered my bare pussy above his face. My knees boxed in his ears.

"Oh, thank you, Nurse Cleo." His grin returned. His tongue reached out.

I raised my hips. "Don't you dare touch my pussy. Lick my ass."

He did as he was told. He laved his tongue around the rim of my anus. I sat my cheeks down right on his nose.

"You are not worthy of this pussy," I said as I

swiveled my hips all over his face, getting him covered in my scent. "But you want it, don't you?"

He couldn't respond with his tongue at work and his face covered. I knew it, but I didn't take it as an excuse. I slapped at his balls when I couldn't hear his response. The flesh of his straining penis was hot and throbbing in the tight cage. His moans of pain sent a thrill through my clit, which is why I didn't realize I'd gone too far until it was too late.

He wasn't allowed to come until I did. And he knew it. But, of course, the bastard shot off before I got there.

A cock cage strains the erection, not allowing it to reach its full potential. It makes coming difficult, but not impossible. West was an overachiever. I looked back as his cramped dick wept its pleasure.

"You greedy, little slut."

"Fuck," he sighed with a sated grin. His head lolled back as he continued to come down from that subspace high and noted the mess he'd made. "Aw," he chuckled. "I'm sorry, Cleo."

"What did you just call me?"

He blinked as though I'd awakened him from a wet dream. "Aren't we done? The scene, or what-ever, is over."

He was done. I hadn't come yet. In fact, I hadn't

come for weeks since I'd been playing around with him. The last time I came was the first time we'd fucked. The first time I'd broken him by sticking my fingers in his ass in the hospital supply closet.

That orgasm had been great. So great that I'd been chasing after it for the last two weeks. Tonight, just like the last half-dozen times I'd played with him; he'd gotten to the finish line before I'd gone a quarter mile. I prepared to climb off him and end things when there was a knock at the door.

"Dr. West?"

West looked pointedly at the straps on the stirrups. "Let me up, Cleo."

I stayed put, hovering my cunt over his face. A tingle zinged my clit as his eyes widened in true fear.

"Dr. West, are you in there?"

A wide grin spread across my face. "Do you want me to get that for you, Dr. West?" I asked, not quite loud enough to be heard outside the room.

"Yes," West called out to the door. "No," he whispered in a growl at me.

The door rattled. My mouth watered at the possibility of the intrusion. I wasn't an exhibitionist. I just liked the idea of West's terror at being caught in such a compromising position. But the pussy below me had locked the damn door. He was absolutely no fun.

"Can I come in?" said the person outside.

"No," said West. "I'm... tied up at the moment." He yanked at the restraints.

"You're needed in the ER," said the voice.

West's eyes lit. He wasn't only a sexual whore; he was also a surgery whore. "I'll be out in a minute."

He looked pointedly at me. I got up and untied him. I might play with him, but I didn't play when it came to my job. I pulled up my underwear and pants, tossed the latex gloves in the bin, and headed for the door.

"Wait," West called out behind me as he splashed water on his face. "Make sure the coast is clear."

"Yeah," I snorted. "Okay, Scooby."

I tossed up my thumbs and then reached out and turned the doorknob without looking first. If he wanted to hide his true nature, that was him. I didn't do closets.

TWO

I left the exam room and walked into a war zone. It wasn't a war zone like you'd find in the Middle East or Central Africa or even in Eastern Europe. There were no guns. No one wailed. No one was dressed in fatigues or cloth that covered them from head-to-toe.

There were a number of scantily clad girls in neon skirts and threadbare halter-tops. This city was a destination for randy Spring Breakers. So, my first thought was this was a backyard barbecue or beach bonfire gone wrong.

Then I noted that the few guys assembled were in jumpsuits that covered them from head-to-toe. There were smudges on everyone's faces, shoulders, hands and clothes. I wasn't a sports fan, but I knew racecar drivers wore flame retardant suits.

I entered the triage area and took stock. There were only four emergency room nurses on call at this time of day. It was lunchtime. A slow time in the ER. The most we got in at this time were work-related incidents; falls from changing light bulbs, ingesting ink through the mouth, ear, and eyes, even temporary blindness from copy machines.

I sifted through the scantily clad girls and sectioned them off to one side of the room. The major concerns in that mix were minor burns on their bare chests, scrapes on their knees, and soot in their weaves.

The men were a little worse-for-wear with burns on their hands. Some were coughing from possible smoke inhalation. Those I sent off with other nurses to check their ABC's; airway, breathing and circulation. The worst cases would need to be administered oxygen through a mask, but it was likely that most simply needed to breathe some clean air.

I approached a pale man with hair so light-blond it was white. He, too, was in one of the racing suits. There were burn marks along the fabric at his shoulder along with a patch of blood.

"Sir, let me have a look."

He jerked away from my touch like I was a

hissing snake. "Don't touch me you fucking coon. You might give me an infection."

I didn't flinch at his diatribe. I'd been called worse. He didn't hit on my least favorite slur; mutt. Because technically, that's what I was. I was a mix of just about every race from both of my mixed heritage parents, much like my namesake, Cleopatra.

I let him go. Misogynists turned me on because I liked breaking them. Racists made me want to trade my dildos for scalpels. Still, I had a duty to serve anyone who came through those doors.

"I told them to take me to Sisters of Mercy, the Catholic hospital," the racist said. "But they brought me to the fucking ghetto."

He stormed towards the ER doors, holding his shoulder. A small trail of males followed behind him. I caught a swastika on two of their jackets as they turned. Just before they headed out the glass doors of the ER, the doors slammed open and a gurney careened inside.

This blond male's eyes narrowed and his lips quirked. The guy on the gurney turned to him with a glare. The paramedics blocked them as they rushed patient inside. The paramedics began shouting out stats.

I took a look at the guy on the gurney. He was in

one of the racing suits, but his suit was not wholly intact. Fire had made its way into the fabric at his shoulder and leg. His blond hair was pristine, but there were smudge marks on his face.

A girl raced to keep up with the gurney. Her short legs stumbling as they pumped alongside the big men to keep up. Tears streamed down her pretty face as she clasped the injured racer's hand. Her church girl ensemble seemed out of sorts with his devil-may-care looks.

"MK, babe, I promise I'm fine," the blond racecar driver said.

But he didn't sound fine. His voice croaked. He had to pause after every other word. He winced as she touched his shoulder.

I looked him up and down. There was blood on his costume, but I couldn't immediately determine the location of the wound. This case would be where the action was so I latched myself onto the gurney. I grabbed the chart and began the intake. Dr. West wasn't the only medical whore in the building.

"Name," I demanded.

"Crow." The racecar driver grinned at me.

"Real name?"

"His name is Christopher Trent," the church girl, MK, answered in his stead.

I addressed further questions about his identification to her. Once I got the age and details of the patient, I moved onto the important stuff. "Tell me what happened?"

"Car crash."

It wasn't the blond that answered. The voice rumbled on a low vibration that arrowed straight to my clit. The vibration was deep enough that it nearly finished the job that Dr. West hadn't been able to complete. I looked up, and then up some more, into a tall drink of whiskey.

His skin was like lava; the kind that oozes out of a molten chocolate cake. His lips were plump as though he'd been kissing someone very recently. His eyes were hard and intelligent.

"An accident?" I parroted.

Mr. Lava Cake exhaled quietly. "No."

His words were steady, but there was guilt rimmed at the edges of his eyes. My pencil stopped moving as I focused on him. I had the urge to heal that wound.

"You think they ran him into the wall on purpose?" MK's voice went shrill.

"Eagle." The blond patient glared at his dark-skinned friend. It was a warning.

The other man, Eagle, held Mr. Trent's glare,

but Eagle didn't say anything further.

"Mr. Trent, tell me what happened?" I addressed the blond, but my attention was focused on his friend.

"Please call me Crow," said the blond. "I didn't lose control." He tried to sit up, but when he did he winced in pain.

"Lie back," I ordered. "Stay still. You might have a concussion."

"He hit the guard wall really hard," said MK. Her voice was tinged with tears. "And then there was nothing but flames."

"I'm fine, I promise," said Crow.

But I could tell by the way he favored one side of his body that he wasn't. His friend, Eagle, must've seen the same.

"I need to know where it hurts," I said.

"I'm fine," said Crow. "I walked away from it. It was a bad wreck. But I got up and walked away. It's just some scrapes and bruises."

"How fast were you going?" I ignored his macho excuses and began examining him.

"Hundred and twenty," he grinned. "Had it for sure. Smoked them all. Until that idiot lost control of his stick."

"It's safe to say you have a concussion," I said

peering into his eyes. "But there may be more going on. We need to wait for the doctor to examine you."

"You're not the doctor?" asked Eagle.

I looked over at him. "No, I'm a nurse. Nurse Cleo."

Even while his friend was in pain, Eagle was checking me out. I had the urge to preen, to lean over and show him how round my ass was. But I was a professional.

Dr. West came up to us. "I hear there was a racing accident." He grinned with eyes bright like a middle schooler arriving just in time to the schoolyard to watch a brawl.

"Mr. Trent was traveling at an excessive speed and hit a wall." I offered him the chart, but he ignored me.

"How fast?" West asked as he began his own exam.

I grit my teeth. I didn't know if West was intentionally trying to piss me off to get a punishment later, or ignorantly pissing me off to get a punishment later.

"I'm fine," Crow repeated. "It's probably just a concussion, like the nurse said."

"I notice that you're favoring one side and your

breathing is labored," I said. "That could mean you have some trauma to your back."

MK trembled and squeaked. Crow glared at me like he'd done with his friend. Like his friend, it had no effect on me.

"Back injuries are common in car accidents." I turned and addressed West. "So to be safe we should order some x-rays for his back, right Dr. West."

West made some notations on the chart. Then he turned to me without looking at me. "Nurse Cleo, it looks like we're good here. Why don't you get these pain prescriptions worked up for my patient?"

I raised an eyebrow at his tone. Standing next to me, I noted that Eagle did the same.

So, this was purposeful pissation. I had the urge to rattle the cage I had on his cock. Instead, I tried to communicate the world of hurt he would be in when I got him alone.

"Of course, Dr. West," I said as sweet as the asinine in me would muster. "Should I also add an MRI and X-ray for his neck?"

West smiled that fake smile; that condescending smile he gave to patients when he used big medical words. "Do you see that on the chart, Cleo?"

Visions of nipple clamps and ball weights danced in my head.

"Put it on the chart."

West and I both turned to the patient's friend. Eagle's eyes were impassive, but his tone had been implacable.

"I don't see anything that indicates back trauma," said West. "It's probably a waste of money. I don't want you gentlemen to come too far out-of-pocket."

"Don't worry about my pocket," said Eagle. "Worry about my brother. Add the test."

Dr. West bristled at the command in that deep voice. His eyes lost focus for a second. Eagle plucked the chart out of my hand and handed it to West.

West shrugged as he took the clipboard. "It's your money." He made the notation, handed the chart to me, and walked away.

I turned back to the group. "Listen," I addressed Crow. "Do not get off this gurney. Lay back and relax."

"Yes, ma'am." Crow grinned.

I knew I needed to keep my eye on this one. He was trouble.

"He needs to rest." I addressed this to Eagle. "Don't let him move too much. He might feel fine but there could be something else under the surface. Maybe I'm wrong, but I'd rather be sure."

Eagle nodded. Our eyes connected. An understanding passed between us without words. I had a fleeting vision. What would that tall form look like on his knees? Would he come up to my belly button or the underside of my breasts? Would those dark eyes twinkle up at me as I buried his face between my thighs?

The corner of Eagle's mouth ticked up as though he'd read my mind. One eyebrow quirked up as though to say, *try it and see.* I walked passed him refusing to pick up the gauntlet he'd thrown down. I may fuck around with doctors, but I drew the line at patients and patients' sexy friends.

I had ethics; not many, but some.

THREE

After getting his x-rays and a few other tests done, I left Crow resting comfortably in his room with his eagle-eyed brother and his sweet, little girlfriend surrounding him. I walked down the halls to the nursing station.

Along the way, there were a few interns who leered at me. I stared back at them openly challenging them. I had no problem with my reputation at the hospital. West wasn't the first surgeon I'd bagged. Not by a long shot. And he wouldn't be the last.

Not a single one of the green interns interested me. I could break each and every one of them in a night. By morning, they'd be begging me to strap on a cock and shove it wherever I pleased. And, by the reddening of their baby cheeks, each of them knew it. Wanted it without knowing that it was a sexual option for them. But the glimpse at the forbidden made them gulp down that lump of sinful desire. It didn't take long for their eyes to drop along with their lascivious glances.

Yeah, thought so.

In the waiting room, I saw a number of other stragglers from the races. But one group stood out from the bunch. There were two guys there. One was big, like Hulk big. He was tall and dark and very handsome. The other was built like a gymnast; strong upper body and slim, muscular lower body.

Two women hung on the men. The foursome stood in a tight huddle with everyone's hands or shoulders brushing or embracing each one in turn. Unlike the other girls in the waiting room, these two women weren't scantily dressed. Also unlike the other girls who were draped haphazardly on the unengaged men hanging around, the Hulk and gymnast had their hands securely wrapped around the two girls.

It was clear that the foursome were two couples. But it looked like they were more. I knew the body language of lovers, and they were all very familiar with each other.

Swingers, maybe? The 70's fad was making a comeback with the Millennial generation. But instead of the term "swingers" the new breed of twenty-somethings called themselves Polys. I had no delusions about monogamy myself, but I was territorial with the things I considered mine.

The big guy caught my gaze. He took a few steps towards me. I actually considered taking a step back as his massive body blocked my path and my view. His voice was deep and gravelly like a bear who'd stolen a man's voice. "We're Crow's brothers."

He pointed between himself and the gymnast, who upon closer examination I saw was Asian to the Hulk's decidedly Spanish, or maybe Latino, features.

Brothers, he'd said? Definitely polyamorous.

"How's he doing?" asked Latin Hulk.

"He's resting comfortably right now," I assured him. "We're running some tests to be sure we know everything that's going on. We have to wait for the results to come back and then we'll know more."

"When can we see him?" This came from the blonde girl sandwiched between the two males. She looked as though she belonged in a church choir, and not the Southern Baptist kind of an urban community. No, she looked like she would sing hymns in a northern, Protestant church.

It was apparent the brothers of this racing crew had a type. The blonde church girl and the prim and proper brunette, MK, back in Crow's room. But the black woman, with a dangerously-short skirt and fuck-me heels that I had to get my own pair of, didn't quite fit the pattern. Still, she looked entirely comfortable and in place wrapped in the Asian man's arms.

"It'll take another sixty minutes for his tests to come back," I said. "You can go back there to his room. Just try not to get him excited. I need him to rest."

The group headed off. Arms around each other. They looked like a family. I stared after them, crossing my own arms over my chest. I felt a tug at my heart and scratched my chest. My eyes tightened as they turned a corner and went out of my line of sight. I turned away and made my way to the reception area where the other nurses were gathered.

"Cleo, can you sign Judith's card?" asked Midge, an older woman with gray streaked hair. Like most nurses present, Midge had been here for years. She'd gone to nursing school before I was born and had weathered Sacred Heart Hospital when it was a one-story charity hospital run by the church. The hospital had since gone public and taken in any soul regardless of what service they might need, be it contraceptive, sterilization, or abortion.

"I feel like I'm always signing these things," I said, taking the pen from Midge.

Judith, the previous Head Nurse, was retiring. She'd been at the post less than two years. The Head Nurse before that had only lasted nine months. Some were promoted, others moved to bigger hospitals with larger paychecks, and some left on maternity leave and never came back.

"I hope you're applying this time," said Midge. "You would be a shoe-in. You basically run this place anyway."

I shrugged instead of answering. But I knew she was right. Everyone knew she was right. After three years at the hospital, I had finally put my shoe in the ring for the promotion. But I had no intention of making it public yet.

I liked my current job. I didn't care to have any more responsibility than I already had. Being an ER nurse came with its own set of stressors. But my situation at home was getting more and more dire. I needed the money that came with the promotion, and this was the best way I knew to get it.

Still, administration was not my thing. I was a people person. I got off on bossing people around. And I could juggle a number of balls in the air at once. But I liked the freedom of checking out every once in a while. And I definitely didn't feel comfortable with people depending on me; which was ironic since I literally had lives in my hands on a daily basis. But those lives were in and out within a week or so. This would be permanent.

I clenched my fingers around the pen before letting it go. I brought that shaky hand to my forehead and felt a thin sheen of sweat. I took a deep breath and the feeling passed. I had to do this. It wasn't just about me any longer.

"Any messages?" I asked Midge. My voice was hushed as I asked.

She looked through the pile of sticky notes and shook her head.

I sighed with relief. It had been a rough week at home. No calls from home today didn't mean anything. I should probably check in. I reached for my cell phone but a loud snap jerked my head up to attention.

"Nurse."

The thing about nurses is we're not jumpy individuals. We don't startle easy from loud noises or fluids leaking out of various human orifices, or missing body parts. We lift our heads, assess the situation, and then we get to work.

So, when one of the new surgeons came to the nursing station, arms waving, face red, voice barking, we lifted our heads calmly.

He spoke with authority. But one look at his fresh white coat, clean scrubs, and pristine loafers didn't sway a single nurse. Not a single one of our scuffed shoes, or faded scrubs jumped at his command.

"I need a nurse," he demanded.

A few eyes found his. Eyebrows raised or eyes rolled. No patient was in danger of dying, we would know. We'd know it way before he did.

The baby doctor looked around the group like an indignant toddler whose mother gave him Cheerios instead of Fruity O's. I had a sudden urge to break him. I wanted to see what he'd be like when he whimpered and crawled when I wouldn't play with his little wee wee.

"I'll take care of it for you."

The voice didn't surprise any of the nurses. No one even bothered to turn to look at its owner.

Nurse Charity Clarke sauntered up to him in

her size-too-small scrubs that gave a view to her cleavage.

"It's nice to know that some people around here are willing to do their jobs." The baby doctor waved his arm in front of Charity to precede him. Then he stared at the ass she suggestively wiggled as she walked in front of him.

"She gives all of us a bad name," said Midge.

"No," said another nurse. "That's Cleo. Her sleeping around with them like a cliché is what gives nurses a bad name."

I didn't take offense. Especially when it was said with a giggle. "Where else am I going to find a quality lay? I earned my reputation, and I'm not easy. Just ask Dr. Winkler or Dr. James or Dr. West."

The cackling and giggling that always accompanied my antics came to a dead stop, like the needle of a record player shoved to the side. All the nurses turned away, looking down at paperwork.

I felt the prickles at the nape of my neck. I knew West was standing right behind me. I plastered on a smile and turned around.

Sure enough, West stood behind me, glaring. "You're needed."

The command in his voice sent a thrill through me. I had no idea where his anger came from, but it enticed me to follow and see where it led. Hopefully, it would lead down to my sorely neglected clit.

"Yes, Dr. West."

I followed him, excited to free his cock from its cage and ride it. I was surprised he was ready for another round so soon. I followed him down the hall, but he didn't go into our normal restroom, or supply closet, or back stairwell. Instead, he went into my supervisor's office.

That fucking, weak pussy. He held the door open for me. I glared at him as I walked past.

FOUR

"Come on in, you two," said the hospital's Nursing Director, Wanda Steele. "Take a seat."

Wanda was at the same time a tolerant tyrant as she was a laid back micromanager. She'd back up any nurse who had a dispute brought against them by a patient or doctor. But behind closed doors, she'd read you the riot act if you crossed a line that was important to her.

Today, she looked weary around the edges of her eyes. Her usually perfect makeup needed another application. And her wig was slightly askew.

For anyone else, this might be a typical end-of-the-day weariness, but I knew Wanda too well. She was never weary. Unless she was coming down with something. I put a hand on the seat farthest from my boss, but I didn't sit.

"What's this about?" I asked standing my ground.

"Dr. West has filed a complaint about you," said Wanda, a sigh evident in her voice. "He says you countermanded him in front of a patient."

"Can he speak for himself?" I stared West down. He did not meet my eyes. "I made a suggestion based on the information I gained from the patient intake. Are you mad at me for having my patient's best interest in mind? Or are you mad because a patient's family member got in your face?"

Just the thought of that tall, dark and sexy mass of yumminess making West grovel got me wet. I hadn't played a good game of cuckold in a long time. Eagle would be the perfect candidate for such an adventure. And West would make a great pawn to shove around the board.

"You act inappropriately around me. Sexually," West said. His lips pinched together like a baby with a soiled diaper.

"Do you really want to have a conversation about our sex life here?"

West flustered. He flung his arms out in my

direction and turned to Wanda. "You see what I mean about how she's been sexually harassing me?"

"How am I sexually harassing the man I'm dating?"

West turned red. His fists balled. And I kid you not; he stomped his foot. "We are not. I've never taken you out."

"*Out* is not a part of my definition of dating. I'm not interested in watching you eat or hearing your opinion on a movie. We're fucking. That doesn't require going out anywhere." I cocked my head and reexamined him. "Unless there's some exhibitionist tendencies you haven't told me about?"

West turned to my superior and pointed his shaking finger at me. "Do you see what I mean? I can't work like this."

Wanda looked between the two of us impassively. She rubbed at her temple with one hand and reached for a slip of paperwork with the other. "According to this, it appears that you two are dating."

"What is that?" West asked, lowering his finger and advancing to Wanda's desk.

"It's the report Nurse Williams filed with HR indicating that you two are seeing each other, and have been for the past three weeks." Wanda handed him the paperwork.

West jerked back as though the sheet of paper was poisonous. "I never filled that out."

"No, I did."

Whenever I was having a sexual relationship with a doctor in the hospital I always made certain to file with HR. Partially to protect myself in situations like these. But also to see them fluster when they got caught. I turned to West and his red face.

"Don't worry," I said, taking the paper from Wanda. "I'll rip that up. It's no longer needed since this relationship is now over."

West squirmed. I wasn't sure if it was because he didn't want our relationship to end? It didn't matter. He no longer had a choice. He was a selfish lover. He'd given me the equivalent of blue balls twice now in one night. He'd already done the whole flustered at being caught thing that I so enjoyed watching. There wasn't any other way I could think to amuse myself with him. So, it was over.

""Would you excuse us, Dr. West," said Wanda. "I'd like a private word with Nurse Cleo."

West's indecision at the ripping of the paperwork dissolved. A smirk spread across his face as though he sensed he'd gotten me into trouble. I narrowed my eyes at him, and his lips twitched until the weight of my glare pulled the corners down into a cowing frown.

Yeah, it was so over between us. West shuffled out the door and I turned back to my supervisor. Wanda shook her head at me once we were alone.

I sat down in the chair, but scooted away from her as she pulled out a tissue and dabbed at her nose. "You coming down with something?"

"I'm fine," she waved my concern away. "You know you're a shoe in for this promotion, Cleo. But I can't promote you with your behavior. You have to set a good example socially as well as professionally."

"You know that's a double standard. Doctors screw nurses all the time. You never see them getting called for their behavior."

"Because we're nurses. We have to set ourselves above those egomaniacs. You've been with us for three years. This is the first time you've applied for a promotion even though you would've been given the position years ago. What's going on? What's changed?"

I wasn't about to tell her the truth. I wasn't about to tell any one I worked with the truth. "I need a new challenge."

Wanda studied me, seeing right through me, but

not the truth. "Fine. But you have to know that your reputation precedes you. If you really want this position, then you have to clean up your act with the doctors."

I shrugged. Doctors were just a pastime. They were an easy habit to break.

Inwardly, I smirked at my own joke. Outwardly, I nodded to Wanda. I couldn't afford to let this opportunity slip by me. Not with Toy getting worse and our time running out.

"I hear you," I said. "He's the last one. I promise."

"Cleo, I know how good you are, but if you want this promotion you have to realize that the doctors also have a say."

"What? So they're gonna try and cockblock me? That's not fair. Any relationship I've had has been on file to avoid exactly this situation."

"It's still a boys' club, hon. Just stop fucking with them."

"Charity fucks with them."

"But she doesn't turn them into whining little girls." Wanda coughed and grabbed for another tissue.

"You should go home and get some rest."

She waved me, and whatever ailed her, away. I

sighed and got up to head out the door. Of course West was waiting for me on the other side like the lap dog he truly was.

"What were you thinking filing a report with HR?" he demanded.

"What's the matter?" I smiled sweetly. "Were you embarrassed about our relationship?"

"What relationship? We were fucking."

I nodded patiently. "Those are the only kinds of relationships I have with men. Did you think it was something else?"

"You're a coldhearted bitch, you know that?"

My head cocked to the side, like the safety being flung off a gun. My gaze narrowed at him, like I was looking at him down a barrel. "Call me a bitch again."

I watched him muster the courage. Then the bastard uttered the word.

I nodded slowly as I looked up and down his body for the perfect place to strike. My gaze latched onto his groin, and I grinned. I took the key from in my ear, the key that fit his cock ring, and placed it in my mouth. Knowing full well that I would regret this in a few hours, I swallowed. Luckily, I had no gag reflex. The piece of metal tumbled down my throat.

West gulped and then grabbed at his stomach as

though he were about to vomit. "What did you...? How am I...?"

Exactly. It was gonna be a bitch on the way out, but damn it if it wasn't worth it for the look on his face.

"Kiss my ass," I said and turned on my heel. But I didn't get far. I walked into a mountain of hard muscle.

"Excuse me." The tall drink of water that called himself Eagle stood in my path. "We need a doctor"

"What's wrong?" both West and I asked.

Eagle ignored West and addressed me. "My brother, he's losing feeling in his arm. He says not to worry about it, but I'm worried."

"It's probably nothing," said West.

"Or it's a spinal fracture," I said.

West turned to me. "Didn't we just have this conversation about you overstepping your bounds?"

I shut my mouth, which was hard for me to do. But I thought about that promotion.

"How do we know if it's a fracture?" Eagle asked.

"The x-rays," said West. "They should be back in thirty minutes."

"We need to put a rush on those," said Eagle.

"I can go and see," I said.

We headed down to the x-ray room. Eagle followed close behind. I felt him stalking behind me like a tiger. I knew his attention was on his friend, but my ass felt a hot gaze. When I chanced a glance over my shoulder, my suspicion was confirmed.

His lazy, hazel eyes were locked on the sway of my ass. He looked up and I was the one who felt like I'd been caught staring.

West opened the door to the x-ray room. He made to close it in my face, but I moved past him. Eagle did the same. West bit his lip and stayed mute.

In the room, two bodies were clasped together in a corner. They sprang apart as we entered. I saw Nurse Charity's bare flesh from her rucked up scrubs, and I got a glimpse of what the new surgeon was working with. I felt a moment's pity that I wouldn't get to play with his toy.

"Excuse me, no patients in here," said the surgeon, his eyes looked past me and West to focus on Eagle.

Eagle glared. If it was possible, he seemed to grow larger in the small room while the new surgeon appeared to shrink. Eagle turned to me. He raised an eyebrow. Then he tilted his head. The silent command indicated that I should get to the business at hand; his friend's x-ray.

"Where's the tech?" I asked. "We need to rush an x-ray. It's an emergency."

"He went down the hall, but I can find it. Patient's name?" The surgeon was all professionalism now.

I told him the name and he pulled the slides. He put them up in the light.

"Dr. Page," said West addressing the new surgeon. It was the first time he'd spoken in the ordeal. "Shouldn't we wait for the tech?"

"I can read an x-ray, West."

We all stared at it for a silent moment, but there was tension in that moment. Namely from West and Page as they each raced to find any evidence in the film. West spoke first.

"Just as I said, there's nothing broken," said West.

"What about any fractures?" I asked.

"He wasn't exhibiting the signs," West insisted.

"Right here," said Page.

West grit his teeth as he glared at the back of Page's head.

"It's a hairline, but it's in the neck," said Page. "It could lead to a spinal problem. Has the patient experienced any numbing in the arms or dizziness?"

"Yes," Eagle spoke up. "He said his arm was feeling numb and he had a headache."

West peered closer. "It looks like he'll need immediate surgery. Let's get him prepped."

Eagle put a hand on West's chest. He didn't shove. He just stopped the man's motion. "Not you." He turned to Page. "You."

Doctors were a competitive bunch, surgery whores as I mentioned, so of course Page jumped at the chance to operate on any live body. "Nurse Charity, come with me."

"I want Nurse Cleo working with you," said Eagle.

Page looked over at me and shrugged. "The more the merrier."

We rushed out the room and down the hall to Crow's room. Page explained the procedure as Crow's brothers looked on with grim faces and each of the three girls' lips trembled.

As we were leaving the room with Crow on a gurney, Eagle made to follow. I pressed my hand against his chest. He was solid steel beneath my fingers. I felt his heart beating; fast and strong. Even though his face was stoic, it was crystal clear that he was worried about his brother.

"I'm sorry, you can't come," I said. "But I

promise you, I'm going to take good care of your brother. I'll be by his side, watching over him every minute."

Eagle's large hand covered mine. I couldn't remember the last time a man had taken my hand in his own with or without my permission. It seemed like he held it there for an eternity, but I knew it was only a second.

He nodded and then stepped back and let me go. My legs took a moment to move. Then I disappeared into the surgery room.

FIVE

I walked out of the surgery room three hours later, which was five hours after my shift should have ended. In the waiting room, I saw that Eagle had Crow's girlfriend in his lap. MK's eyes were open but vacant. Eagle's hand stroked across her back where her bra strap would be.

The others were similarly seated together, holding one another close and offering support. This multihued, multiethnic group looked like a patchwork from afar. Up close, they made complete, harmonious sense. I wrapped my arms around myself, wishing I had a blanket to snuggle into.

As I came closer, Eagle's gaze connected with mine. His eyes widened and I saw fear and vulnerability glare through in his hazel depths. I held up my hand in a stop motion, trying to indicate that everything was okay.

His eyes closed for a second. His fingers tensed on MK's back. She didn't notice. I held up my thumb, pointing it towards the sky in the universal signal of *Everything's Okay*. His eyes closed again. In that moment I was free to look my fill of him.

I drank in the sight of him sitting there, vulnerable with another woman in his lap. I liked the picture very much. I wanted him on his knees, head tilted back at me, eyes closed, lips parted. Oh, the things I'd stick in that mouth.

Eagle's eyes flashed opened. They caught and held mine like he knew what I was thinking. Even though his eyes were open, I couldn't tell what he was thinking. I doubted this man had a submissive bone in his body. Unfortunately, that made me want him even more. It would likely take a lifetime to break him. But oh, during that time, I could make him hurt so good.

His eyebrow quirked in a challenge. I stuttered in my steps as I came to stand before him. My fight or flight response engaged. Something told me that another step forward would put me in a trap. A step backwards would get me chased. I wasn't a pussy and so I stepped forward.

The side of his mouth quirked up as I did. I couldn't tell what things he wanted to do to me, or wanted me to do to him. I couldn't read his kink, other than he was the type who liked to share. I knew he had to see that I wasn't the type of woman who was a toy. I was a toymaker.

He gave the woman in his lap a light tap. MK looked up. She blinked and slowly her gaze came into focus. She regarded Eagle, her eyes full of trust as she waited for further instructions from him.

That pulled me up short. I'd never had that; trust in a man. Or a woman for that matter. I didn't have some tragic childhood where a man abused me and that was why I liked to hurt them. I was an equal opportunity sadist. I spared the church girl's ass a moment of perusal as she stood to allow Eagle up, wondering what shade her skin would blush if handled correctly.

The other two men and their women stood as well. They all approached me as a unit. Each man and woman fanned out, surrounding me. The final formation wasn't a U shape that left me at the head. It was a circle, which included me.

"The surgery went well," I said. "He's resting comfortably."

A collective sigh of relief went through the

group. MK's trembling hands were collected up by the Asian man. The blonde woman wrapped her arms around MK's torso lending further support.

I had given many families good news. I'd given my share of bad news, too. But I'd never felt included the way I did in the midst of this group. It left me with a sense of unease. I took a step back.

"The doctor will be out to tell you more, soon."

Before I could take another step in retreat, Eagle stopped me with a feather light touch on my elbow. "Will you tell us your prognosis?"

He didn't tug me. He barely had a hold on me. But somehow I found myself taking two steps forward and back into the circle of the group.

He released his hold on me and I was sorry for it. I liked this man more and more with each word he said to me. Visions of a gag shoved into his mouth danced through my mind.

"You were right to push for the x-rays," I said. "It was a fracture. If we had let it go, your brother could've had permanent spinal damage. You probably saved his life."

Eagle was silent. I could see his jaw working. The expression on his face reeked of guilt and shame. I wanted to take my words back, but I didn't know which ones had elicited that response. I'd hoped to make him feel prideful, vindicated.

"He's going to be fine," said the blonde girl who was wrapped around MK. She put her arms around Eagle and squeezed. He turned his head and kissed her temple absently, but his eyes remained on me.

I took a moment to take in the blonde again. She did not look like the type to be shared, but I knew from experience that it was usually the quiet girls that were the freaks. They were my favorite.

I liked my men to be assholes that I would break down into weepy little girls. I liked my women to be good girls that I could turn into kinky little toys at my beck and call. When the blonde's blue gaze met mine, I knew I could have her sucking my toes, my nipples, and then my clit in under an hour.

She jerked away from Eagle with a gasp and blinked at me. She knew it, too. The way she bit her lip told me I was probably wrong —it would likely only take ten minutes.

Beside her Eagle grinned, the shame and guilt dropped from his face and he let out a low chuckle as I sized up his companion and she lowered her gaze submissively.

"Good news, folks." Doctor Page's smug tone broke the spell. "Your buddy is going to be okay. As you know, I caught the fracture early enough in the x-rays and I was able to repair the damage. Mr. Trent will need to stay here and rest for a few days, but I expect a full recovery."

Everyone nodded at the doctor's words, but all eyes stayed on me. Each one of Crow's family members came up and thanked me, giving Page a cursory nod before turning to gather their things from the waiting room.

"I'm going to stay," said MK.

"I'm sorry," I said. "Only family can stay the night."

"They're engaged," said Eagle.

That surprised me. Most polyamorous groups I'd encountered didn't put any weight on legal partnerships.

"That counts," I said. "He's in post-op right now, but you can wait for him in his room, okay?"

"Thank you," she said.

She came up and embraced me. I felt her inhale and then slowly exhale. I rubbed her back. She gave me a brave smile as she let me go.

"Thank you," she repeated.

I nodded and turned on my heel. My legs were a bit shaky as I walked away. Again, I felt dark, smoldering eyes on my ass. But when I turned around, they were all gone.

I finally had a few minutes to myself. I clocked out before anyone could ask me to do anything else. I went into the locker room for my things. Checking my phone, I saw that there were no missed calls or messages. That was rare.

I swiped at my phone and dialed the contact marked TOY. I tried not to get nervous when it rang the fourth and then fifth time. But on the sixth ring there was the clicking sound of a connection.

"Hello?" said a groggy voice.

"Hey, baby girl." I sighed with relief. "Did I wake you?"

I could hear her inhale, pushing the crust of sleep from her body. "You're still at work?"

"I'm leaving now. Just wanted to check on you. You had a good day?"

I heard her take another inhale. There was the creaking of a mattress as I assumed she tried to sit up in her bed. "There was a delivery guy. He knocked even though we signed that leave package form. I used the intercom and he left the package outside. I'm sorry, but it's still there."

"That's okay, baby. I'll get it on my way in."

"And there's a problem with the cable again."

"I'll schedule a tech to come out on my next day off."

"What time is it?"

It was seven in the morning, the start of a new day. Toy did well at night. It was the days that she often had trouble with.

"What happened?" she asked. "Why'd you stay so late? Was there some major accident the ER had to handle? Or did you get caught up under some doctor?"

"Both."

"Dr. Douche? Did he earn out of his chastity belt?"

I inhaled through my nose and scrubbed at my face.

"Uh oh, what did he do?" I could hear the laughter in her voice. It sounded good. This was my favorite version of Toy; happy and giggly. The anxious, fearful one was still asleep on the mattress.

"The idiot tried to tattle on me to my supervisor. So, I swallowed the key to his cock cage."

There was silence. And then Toy burst out laughing. "You're right, he is an idiot. I know better."

"Yes, you do."

"Because I'm a good girl."

"Yes, you are."

She purred into the phone like a kitten. I had the urge to race home and scratch behind her ears, rub her belly, and pet her in that special place.

"Anyway," I said as I closed my locker. "I'm done with doctors."

Toy laughed again. "You've said that before. And then a new jerk comes on the scene and you can't help but put his balls in a vise."

"I can't afford to anymore. We need the money."

She was silent for a moment. "It's my job to do the worrying in this relationship."

"It's my job to make things better so that you don't have to worry. That's what I'm doing now. Okay?"

"Yes, Mistress."

"Good girl. I'll be home soon. Do you need anything?"

"No, I put in an order with the grocery store and Amazon. Those should arrive this afternoon while you're home."

"All right. Then I want you to get up, take a shower, and wash that pretty kitty of yours."

"Yes, Mistress."

I caught the catch in her voice and it made me smile. "Good girl."

I got off with Toy. I wished I'd used my break to

take a nap instead of play around with West, or Dr. Douche as Toy had so aptly labeled him. Instead, I was left frustrated and with a bout of indigestion. Still, it was a new day and I was making a fresh start.

Or so I thought, until I turned the corner and another cleansing product blocked my path.

SIX

"There you are, Nurse Cleo."

"Actually, there I go, Dr. Page. I'm heading out."

"You did a great job in there," he said, ignoring my words. He rounded me, blocking my path, and leaned in.

People who were bigger than me always made the mistake of thinking that their size would intimidate me. I stared Page down with a glassy gaze, cold and unblinking. His confident smirk faltered. I raised an eyebrow and cocked my head, indicating that he should get down to business.

"I saw you've been having some trouble with Dr. West."

I sighed and rolled my eyes. I knew exactly where this little caring speech was headed.

Page cleared his throat and straightened his white coat. His eyes softened into predatory slits and his voice regained a false sense of confidence now that my glare was focused upwards.

"I have a solution," he said. "I think it would be mutually beneficial if we worked more closely together. I'd like to take you under my wing."

"I'm not interested in flying, thank you." Giving him a curt smile that cut at the inside of my lips, I made to step around him.

Page blocked my path. Big mistake. But Wanda's words to play nice went through my ears. I rolled my neck. The cracking of the tendons in my neck worked to slow my mouth down from saying something stupid.

"You should consider it," Page said. "I know you're up for a promotion alongside Nurse Charity. The report I give could influence the decision depending on how well we work together."

I'd seen his work with Charity in the x-ray room. The next crack I heard were my knuckles. Luckily, I'd only balled my hand into a fist. It didn't connect with anything on his body —yet.

I looked Page up and down. It wasn't a long journey. It would be so easy to break this man. He had mama's boy written all over him. He was of that breed of Millennials that had everything handed to him. The kind of kid that was taught to the test and not to think for themselves. The kind of kid that had been praised for just participating in the game and given a trophy for showing up.

It would take me a day, two max, before I was in his ass with a monster cock and he was begging me for more. It would be so very easy.

I took a step back. "Dr. Page, both you and my supervisor will have to judge my work based on my merits. Between Nurse Charity and I, I'm sure the best woman will win."

Page looked up at the ceiling, as though he ran my words over in his head again and again. Then his jaw ticked when he realized he'd been rejected. "You've fucked every doctor in this place. You think you're too good for me?"

"Honey, I would be so bad for you." I reached out and patted him on his smooth, hairless chin. "I would turn you into my bitch and you would give me your job. But I don't have the time or the energy to play with you and work through your homoerotic tendencies right now. I need to get home."

"Oh yeah." He tilted his baby chin up and down. "I heard you were a lesbian."

"Sure," I said. "If that makes you feel better."

"Cleo?"

I caught sight of Wanda in the distance. Dr. Page took two steps to the side of me as she came to join us.

"You're supposed to be long gone," said Wanda.

I wanted to say the same to her. Her nose was red and her eyes puffy. I knew that if I fussed, she'd brush my concern away. From years of nursing I could tell that whatever had taken a shot at her would knock her down soon enough.

"Mrs. Steele, I'm glad you're here," said Page. "I just wanted to tell you what a valuable asset I think Nurse Charity is. Her help was instrumental on the surgical floor today. Not only that, but she caught a mistake another doctor had made."

Wanda looked to me. "Is that so?"

I remained mute. I was too tired to play this game. "I'll see you both tomorrow."

"Cleo," called Wanda. "Are you on the schedule later tonight?"

"No, I'm off. I'm going to spend the day with my girlfriend. We've got some lesbian stuff to do."

I rounded the corner, thinking I'd escaped any more roadblocks when I walked into a wall of a chest. What the hell? Was I a magnet for man boob today?

There was no flab on this chest. It was all muscle and sinew and sin. Eagle reached out and steadied me. I took a step back and met the wall. I didn't like men caging me in. I always had the upper hand. I resented that I had to look up so far. I'd felled men taller and broader than him. But there was something about the rock hard presence of him that seemed impenetrable. Damn, I wanted to climb that wall.

Eagle stepped back and gave me room to breathe. "You headed out?"

"Yeah, my shift is over. Was over before your friend's surgery. But..."

"Thank you for that."

"You don't have to thank me. It's my job."

"Don't do that." He gave a forceful shake of his head to accompany his directive. The command in his voice called me up short. "You and I both know who did their job today."

I didn't answer. He didn't need me to. A man like him didn't need to see any recommendations or reports. He'd likely looked at me while I was doing his brother's intake and made up his mind.

"Can I ride down the elevator with you?" he asked.

"I'm taking the stairs."

He held out his hand for me to precede him. I headed into the stairwell.

"I owe you," he said as the door shut behind us.

"No, you don't," I said, bracing my hand on the rail to steady myself. "The hospital pays my bills."

"I wasn't offering cash."

I turned and caught those hazel eyes. I knew exactly what he was offering before he spat out the words. My steps halted, but I kept my grip on the railing.

"So, is there anything else you might need?" he asked.

His voice was a purr. There was a gulf of space between us, but I felt like those words reached out and pinched my tits. I pressed my thighs together.

"Anything at all you might need?" He was beside me, but he took a step down below me, so that he had to peer up into my face.

His head tilted back. His lips parted. There was a hint of vulnerability on his face, just a hint. He let me look. Fuck if I didn't want to wrench his head back and expose his Adam's apple.

My panties dampened as I looked down at him in the submissive pose he'd struck. He inhaled as though he knew my juices scented the air, the bastard.

"Just ask," he said. "And I'll give it to you."

How did he know I needed to come so bad? I'd been denied by Doctor Douche earlier. I hadn't had a good orgasm in days. I couldn't remember the last time a guy had worked me over enough to elicit something from my pussy, but I knew this guy could. If I let him.

"It looks like you need something," he said, "and I'd really like to give it to you."

A door above us opened and voices poured down. It broke the trance. Thank god.

"Too many people use this stairwell." That was not what I meant to say. I'd meant to deny him out right.

"We can go somewhere else."

I shook my head. "An orgasm is not on the invoice."

"It would just be between us."

I shook my head, slowly, left to right. I swore I heard it creak against the pressure. "I'm taking a break from men."

He grinned sadly, taking another step down, putting himself in an even more submissive stance. Did he know what he was doing to me?

"As you wish," he said. He stepped back into the railing, giving me a wide berth to pass.

It took a few seconds for my legs to work. I gripped the railing on both sides as I made my way down. He followed at a respectable distance.

"You guys are race car drivers?" I tried to change the subject.

"Yeah."

We reached the ground floor and stepped out into the sunlight. "What happened on the track? You don't seem to think it was an accident."

Eagle turned his face into the sun. I didn't think he was going to answer. We were at my car by the time he spoke.

"It was a bump and run," he said.

"That sounds kinky."

He gave me a half smile, but his eyes were still far away, probably back at the racetrack. "It's when a car that's behind you taps your bumper. It makes you slow down and then the other car can speed past you."

"Sounds like cheating to me."

He nodded. "Yeah."

"Did the other driver get hurt?"

He nodded again. "Minor wound. He went to a different hospital."

I remembered the blond haired racist and his merry band of Nazis that had stormed out of the ER as Crow was being brought in. "Are you guys pressing charges?"

"The track officials are investigating it now. What will most likely happen is he'll be slapped with a fine and have to sit out one or two races."

Something in the tense set of his jaw told me that that wouldn't be the end of it. I just hoped that whatever he, and the rest of his brothers, were planning didn't end him up in my ER again.

"Your brother is going to be okay," I said.

"Thanks to you." He gave me a soft smile. Any thoughts of violence wiped clean from his handsome face.

"Thanks for walking me to my car." I unlocked the door and slid into the driver's seat. He shut it for me and leaned against the frame as I turned over the ignition.

The car wheezed. I tried again. It coughed. The last thing I needed was a car repair bill on top of the other crushing debt that Toy and I were under.

I jumped at the knock on the window. Eagle smiled and made a motion for me to roll the window down. I did.

"I can fix that, too," he said once there was no longer glass between us.

My hand turned the ignition again. This time

the engine kicked over. I grinned triumphantly at Eagle. His smile was filled with patience.

"You let me know when you change your mind, Nurse Cleo."

"*When* I change my mind?"

His answer was a patient smile that touched his eyes, accenting his flaring nostrils.

In response to that carnal invitation, I flipped him the bird.

"Please," he said.

My finger wobbled. I was a sucker for making a grown man beg. He chuckled like he knew my kink and was playing with me. I rolled up the window and took off. That guy was dangerous. I pressed the gas and put as much distance between us as fast as I could.

SEVEN

I pulled into our cul-de-sac. It wasn't exactly a cul-de-sac. It was a dead end street that curved into a patch of dirt between two houses. To call it a blue collar neighborhood would be too kind.

The neighborhood was ninety-eight percent white. There had been one black family that had lived here years ago, but the son sold the house to a young white family after his parents passed away. So, the remaining two percent was me. And then you could cut that down to about a quarter of a percent because I didn't come from a family of purebreds.

My English-born mother had tasted the rainbow and come out the other side with a colorful set of children. Not one of the three of us shared the same daddy or the same heritage. None of us currently shared the same continent. My mum had gone back to England a decade ago. My older brother, Khan, was backpacking through Asia. And my younger brother, Solomon, went into the Peace Corp in the Middle East.

I saw another for sale sign as I drove down the single lane street. Most homes had for sale signs, but no one was buying. A developer was swooping in to get all the properties. Fewer and fewer families were holding out. Demolition had begun just a few streets over.

I pulled up to our house and hit the brakes. There was a car in my driveway. I knew that car. Goddamn Ford, American-made car that guzzled gas and polluted the airways. What the hell was she doing here?

The she in question stormed out of my house, throwing the door wide open. She reached for the handle, but then smirked and left the door open.

I saw red.

She saw me.

She made a mad dash for her rusty car and climbed in. I pulled up to the back of the driveway blocking her. I saw her blue eyes narrow in the rear view mirror in a challenge. My nostrils flared as I revved my engine.

She leaned out of the car window, torquing her body to face me. "Move out of the way, you fucking mutt."

I rolled my window down to be sure she could hear me. "Hit me, bitch."

We sat in this close-proximity game of chicken for thirty seconds. I honestly don't know who moved first. She backed up and I gunned it. The crash wasn't as loud as I'd hoped, which left me feeling unsatisfied. It was more of a crunch as her tinfoil car slammed into the steel of my German-built car.

Lisa hopped out of her car. She raced around to her rear bumper. When she got there she pulled the ends of her hair with tight fists and let out a string of curses.

I got out too, and surveyed the damage on the front end of my car. Where her bumper was mangled mine had a dent. I patted my car, good girl. In answer, smoke seeped out of the hood. Shit, that was going to cost me.

"What the fuck is wrong with you?" Lisa shouted. "Are you retarded, too?"

"Get off my property," I growled.

"It's my property." She pointed her thumb to her chest. "My mother left it to me and that freak in there."

I took a step toward her, my voice low and menacing. I itched for a flogger to punish her ass, but then clamped down on the thought. This bitch didn't deserve the pleasure my pain could give her. "Don't call her that."

"Victoria was doing fine before you came here. So was my mother."

"You're just mad I didn't come sniffing around your panties."

Lisa turned red. She sputtered and flustered, shaking her head. But along with her head shaking, her whole body gave an unfulfilled shudder. Another confirmation of my theory that most homophobes were secretly curious.

"You nasty, nig-," Lisa spat.

I took a menacing step towards her before she could get out the rest of that heinous word. She jerked back.

I didn't have the same theory about racists that I had about homophobes. I truly doubted that they secretly wanted to be a part of the race they denigrated. The insult should've rolled off me. I'd heard it so many times that they'd lost their power, especially after I realized how much she secretly and shamefully wanted me.

I couldn't tickle her clit with insults right now. I was operating on no sleep in almost three days. I looked at the damage I'd done to her car. That would have to be enough for today. I'd pay her back for the slur the next time we crossed paths, which was hopefully never. I just wanted her out of my way right now. I rounded her and headed for the door to the house.

"You need to sell this house and get off welfare," Lisa yelled.

"I'm a nurse," I threw over my shoulder. "I make more in a night than you do in a week."

"Then buy me out."

She had me there. I didn't have that kind of cash on hand. And even if I did, I couldn't sell this place. It was Toy's safety net. I was at the top of the stoop when I turned around to glare at her.

"Don't you care at all for your sister? She's your family."

Lisa's lip curled. "She can leave that house; she's just being a brat. You have until the end of the month to come up with the money or you have to sell. Doesn't matter to me which way."

Lisa hopped into her car. She backed out into the grass to get around my car and onto the street. Before she gunned it, she threw her middle finger up and then she sped down the street.

I looked at the dent in my car. It wasn't so bad. It was the smoke coming out of the hood that worried me. I'd have to pay for that now. Smart, Cleo.

I left the car where it was; half in the driveway. I doubted it would start so that I could move it. The neighbors didn't bother coming out to see what the matter was. It wasn't that kind of street.

I scooped up the package on the porch, rushed into the house, closing and then locking the door behind me. "Victoria?" I called out softly.

She didn't make a peep. I found her sitting at the top of the stairs, just behind the stairwell. She was curled into a ball with her arms wrapped around her knees. Her eyes were shut so tight her eyelashes touched her cheeks.

"Toy, baby. I'm here."

I touched her softly, with my fingertips at first.

"Victoria, open your eyes."

"I th-thought it w-was the cable g-g-guy," she said. She rocked faster and her eyes stayed closed. "I came d-down the steps and opened the door and everything. You were g-gonna be so p-proud of me."

"I am, baby." I stroked her long, wheat-colored hair out of her face. "Look at you. You're out in the hall. You're not locked in the bathroom."

Toy took a deep breath. Her hands relaxed enough for me to curl my fingers around hers. But she didn't open her eyes.

"The door is closed, baby. She's gone."

"She said she's gonna sell. Gonna kick us out. Out. Out." Toy began hyperventilating and rocking again. Her fingers gripped mine and her arms clenched around her knees.

"That's not gonna happen, baby. I won't let it."

She shook her head. "I can't go out. Out. Out."

"Toy. Stop it." I put every ounce of bass in my voice that I had.

Toy stopped talking. She shut her mouth, but she didn't stop rocking. I knew she was trying to break through, trying to master herself. My heart clenched to watch her struggle.

"Count your primes," I commanded.

She nodded her head. She took a few deep breaths. Her rocking slowed but didn't stop.

"Now, Toy."

"Two...three...five...seven..."

"Good girl. Get on your knees."

She unfurled her arms and came to her knees. She wore a pair of loose jogging shorts and a tank top. "...twenty-nine...thirty-one..."

"Good girl. Keep counting."

Victoria was a theoretical mathematician. She'd gotten her degree from MIT via their online campus. She had some contracts with international think tanks but her condition didn't make her the most reliable employee. Most of her contracts were paid after completion of the work. She didn't always make her deadlines, which meant she didn't always get her fees. But still, clients came back to her again and again because the woman had a beautiful mind.

"...seventy-nine...eighty-nine...Ah!"

Toy lurched forward. Her partially bare ass cheeks clenched. Her eyes closed and her head dipped back.

I shook my head after stinging her ass with my open hand. "Did you forget something?"

She took a deep breath and settled back down. She recounted. "Seventy-nine, *eighty-three*, eighty-nine..."

"Good girl." I pulled the elastic of her shorts all the way down exposing her creamy ass.

Toy gasped as the cool air hit her bare skin. Her

blue eyes clouded over like a rainy day. Her pink lips parted on a soft sigh.

Good. She was in the present moment.

I rubbed her ass in soft circles, feeling her shake in anticipation of the next whack. Her counting slowed. I gave her a slap. "Did I say stop?"

"No, Mistress." She began the sequence again.

Anxiety disorder was a bitch of a disease. It could attack people in many ways and go undetected. When I met Victoria it was as her mother's in home nurse. I tried to hold my tongue as her mother yelled at the poor girl, convinced Victoria was being lazy. It took me just a few weeks to see that Victoria had severe anxiety. The cache of prescriptive drugs she was on made her lethargic and shiftless. But after I caught her watching me beneath a hooded gaze, I knew exactly what she needed. A firm hand.

I slid my fingers between her ass cheeks and into her wet cunt.

"Squeeze," I said.

She did as she was told and squeezed her pussy muscles around the single finger I inserted in her.

"Ah," she yelped as I spanked her with my free hand. I felt her walls quiver as the sting resonated deep inside her.

"You stopped counting," I said.

"Sorry, Mistress."

"Squeeze."

She struggled to do both; count primes and squeeze her pussy walls. The tactic worked. Her mind was on her tasks and not on her worries of the future. I sped up the motions of my finger inside her, finding the thick patch of nerves at the front of her sex. I pushed outward and rubbed hard.

With my other hand, I gave her a firm tap every other prime. She was a shaking quivering mess by the time she got to one hundred and ninety-nine. Her orgasm rocked her body harder than her fear. I cradled her in my arms as she came down.

I loved watching a woman come. There was something about the feminine orgasm that entranced me. A woman's orgasm was so fickle that her release was a coveted dream, an answered prayer. I was blasphemous. I liked being a god.

I viewed male orgasms as selfish acts of completion. But a woman came with her whole body, her spirit, her soul and oftentimes it was only the beginning. Her body opened, allowing a deeper access after each series of contractions.

Victoria was drowsy after coming down. I helped her back to bed and tucked her in for a nap.

Any worries of her bitch of a sister or our money problems were gone by the time I closed her door.

I headed to my own room. I was wired. My body primed for a release of its own, but I was too tired to play with myself. I felt a moment of regret that I hadn't taken Eagle up on his offer.

But it was only a moment, and then I was asleep.

EIGHT

I slept a full twelve hours. When I woke up, I spent an agonizing twenty minutes on the toilet unlocking my bowels. Then I scarfed down the French toast and fresh squeezed orange juice Toy had prepared for me. She was doing well this morning. The cable guy came and fixed the Internet. She'd handled the service visit on her own after I answered the door.

I wanted to feel proud of her, but I was too exhausted. I climbed back in the bed and went back to sleep for another four hours. By the time I opened my eyes again it was time for my next shift.

Rising from the cocoon of my comforter, I felt well rested. I had every intention of going into work and being professional as shit to every doctor, nurse, and patient I encountered. I was working the afternoon shift today and would get to skip the morning rush hour traffic so I took my time getting ready.

With no commuters to fight, I'd make it to work in twenty minutes easy. I kissed Toy goodbye and I walked out the front door. It wasn't until I closed and locked the door behind me that I remembered.

Fuck.

My car sat half in and half out the driveway. To add insult to injury, a citation flapped against the windshield in the light breeze. I pulled out my phone and called an Uber. The ETA on the app said ten minutes.

Thirty minutes later, I walked into the sliding glass doors of the ER. I was ten minutes late. But no one seemed to notice. At the nurse's station, there was a flurry of activity.

"What's going on?" I asked as I stepped into the fray.

"Sisters of Mercy Hospital is here," said Midge. "Sacred Heart is considering a merger."

I cursed out a hiss, pretty apt because a snake was trying to enter my paradise. Sisters of Mercy was a Catholic hospital. Over the last decade, Catholic hospitals across the nation were merging with for-profit and nonsectarian hospitals on a rapid, gluttonous basis. The Catholic hospitals claimed to provide charity care that would serve the poor and uninsured. But that care came at a price; namely the violation of women's reproductive health.

"They brought in a team to tour the facilities to make their final decision."

"Where's Wanda?" I asked.

"She's out sick."

I pinched the bridge between my eyes as a nerve worked in my left eye. Wanda was rarely sick, but of course she'd catch something when a potential virus made ready to infect us all.

"Charity's going to tour them," Midge continued.

That was probably wise. Charity could schmooze the pants off anybody. I wouldn't be surprised if that included a priest. I was not good at holding my tongue when I disagreed with someone. I'd likely tell the delegation every ill thought I had about an organization like theirs.

"If she impresses them, and we do merge, she'll get the supervisor position for sure," I said. "Either way, I think I'd have to leave Sacred Heart. I can't decide which is worse? Being under Catholic Doctrine or being under Charity's management."

"Well, it's not over yet." Midge rubbed my shoulder. "She's bound to fuck up. She always does."

"Yeah, but then she fucks somebody and it all goes away." I picked up a chart and turned from Midge. I barely got a few steps before I hit a wall.

The wall's arms came out and grabbed me. I looked up into bright, hazel eyes set in a dark face. Eagle's skin was smoother than a Hershey's bar and damn me if I didn't want to bite his lips.

"I was wondering where you were," he said, his mouth spreading in a grin.

"Car trouble." My entire body weight was cocooned inside his ropey forearms. My feet were on the ground but my head felt light.

"Want me to take a look?"

"At what?"

His large hands cupped my elbows lightly. My fingertips tingled and the center of my palms warmed.

"Your car," he grinned.

"My car's not here. I had car trouble this morning."

He cocked an eyebrow and grinned while my brain caught up with my mouth and I remembered that I'd said that already.

"It's a long story." I shook my head to clear it and stepped out of his hold. "Why were you looking for me?"

"My brother's been asking for you."

"I've been taking care of Mr. Trent." Charity strolled down the hall, her hips swayed and switched in her tight fitting scrubs. She sidled up to Eagle as though she were waiting for a pat on the head. She eyed the thick candy bar, but when I turned to him, his eyes were still on me.

"I think Crow needs his bed pan changed," Eagle told her. "Would you take care of that for me Nurse Rita?"

Charity bristled. Her eyes narrowed and she grit her teeth like a kid at the front of the class with a raised hand who just got overlooked. But then Eagle turned that charming smile on her.

"Do you think you could do that now?" he asked with that Cheshire-wide grin.

Charity melted on the spot. I swear I saw her panties drip down to her ankle. She giggled and then headed down the hall to take care of Crow's shit.

With Charity on her way, Eagle turned that smile back on me. After that display, I had even more envy for the power of his cock. But I didn't necessarily want it. I had a collection of my own.

"You just got yourself a fan," I said.

"I'm cool." He shrugged. "She doesn't make me hot."

I laughed at the joke. He pulled in his bottom lip. The way his eyes oscillated over my body raised the temperature in my cotton scrubs.

"You need to stop looking at me like that," I said.

"Like what?"

"Like I'm candy on a stick."

His smile dropped in disappointment. "You're not?"

I grinned, but my words were firm. "I told you, I'm not on your invoice. I don't date patients."

"I'm not a patient. But it's no matter, I don't date." He studied me. "Neither do you."

The way this guy read me was uncomfortable.

"You seem to have a lot of doctors interested in you," he said. His gaze was fixed over my shoulder where I saw both Dr. West and Dr. Page sneaking glances as they stood before the surgery board.

I shrugged. "I'm up for a promotion."

"Let me guess; they'll give you their vote of confidence in exchange for... a favor?"

"Something like that." I was insanely curious to know what he had to say to that. When he did speak, it wasn't what I would've expected.

"You're a ladder climber?" He nodded at me with approval. "I like ambitious women. I assume that was your rival? Nurse Fangirl. She giving you trouble, too?"

Eagle inclined his head to Charity who was in Crow's room. I saw Crow grimace as Charity shut the door.

"She gives nurses a bad name, sleeping her way to the top."

Eagle raised one of those eyebrows at me again. I knew he'd seen me yesterday with West and the cock cage key.

"I fuck for fun, not free rides."

He crossed his arms and nodded. "I can respect that."

"But I'm done fucking doctors. Charity can play that game if she wants."

"You need any help? I'm good with games."

I gazed up at him. He held still for my perusal. I had no idea what he thought he could do and I didn't want to find out. Owing a man like Eagle seemed like a dangerous proposition.

"No," I said. "I'll get this promotion on my own merit."

"Nurse Cleo, there you are," said Page, coming over in a huff. "Mrs. Steele is out and I need a nurse to take around the Sisters of Mercy Hospital Delegation."

"I thought Nurse Charity was helping you with that?"

"I can't find her?" Page shrugged as he rubbed a finger against the side of his nose.

"Really?" I said. "I thought she'd attached herself to you."

He balled his hand at his side and pursed his lips. "Do you want to come along or not?"

I was about to point in the direction where he could find Charity, but then I realized this could give me an edge in the promotion. I turned back to Eagle. "I'll be by later to check on your brother, I promise."

Eagle nodded. There was a twinkle in his eye that told me to expect trouble when I found him later. When I turned I felt that heated gaze again on my ass. I may have put a little switch in my step in anticipation of my next run in with that man.

NINE

I followed West down the hall. He stepped ahead, his long strides forcing me to fall behind. It was a power move. I swallowed hard. I didn't want to play with him, I reminded myself. Even if playing meant beating his smug ass to a simpering pulp. I was sticking to the plan. I was on a doctor diet.

"Just smile and nod," West called over his shoulder. "You can handle that, can't you, Nurse Cleo?" He managed to look down his nose at me from the quick glance his profile gave me.

I glared at the back of his head, keeping my pace. I clenched my fingers into fists. I would not crack my open palm against his tight ass like I wanted to.

Up ahead, I saw the members of the Sisters of Mercy delegation. They were easy to discern. The men in the group were in business suits with pinched looks on their faces. The women, the two of them present, were dressed in habits and coifs; nuns.

I saw the Chief of Staff, Gary Rowe. His salt and pepper head bobbed enthusiastically at the stoic congregation. Chief Rowe was smiling and schmoozing. He was in his natural habitat. He looked up and his smile slipped a fraction when he saw me. I'd made him my bitch my first year here. His gaze diverted to the ground and he straightened his tie.

I focused my attention on the two women in the group. The older nun looked down her nose at me even though I was taller than her. She'd read me right, I couldn't disagree. I was worse than Mary Magdalene.

The younger nun held no judgment in her eyes, though I know she had assessed me, too. She had the cool gaze of a trained nurse. But she kept the diagnosis to herself waiting for the older nurse to make the prognosis.

"This is Dr. Page," said Chief Rowe. "He is one of our promising surgeons."

The gentlemen shook Dr. Page's hand. Then they turned their attention to me. There was a brief, awkward silence when it wasn't clear whether or not I'd get an introduction.

"And this is Nurse Cleo," Page filled the gap. "She's going to show you the Emergency Room floor, which is the heart of what we do here at Sacred Heart for our neighbors in the surrounding community."

I smiled and offered my hand. I was careful to keep my grip light against all of their soft, fleshy palms. I saw pupils dilate as each male gaze connected with mine. They'd read me right, too.

When I got to the nuns I wasn't sure if I should shake hands or not. What was the protocol with holy women? The young nurse held out her hand.

"I'm Sister Ruth."

Sister Ruth's hands were pale white, but her skin was rough as though they'd seen many a hard day's work. I liked her instantly.

"And this is Sister Mary Helena," Sister Ruth offered.

Sister Mary Helena did not hold out her hand. She gave me a barely perceptible nod.

"Nurse Cleo," said Chief Rowe. "As you may have heard, Sacred Heart Hospital is considering merging with Sisters of Mercy Hospital. It would be a boon to the ER and our mission to help the less fortunate in our great city, which I know has been one of your passions as you've moved up the ranks of hospital staff."

Rowe was baiting me. The only rank I'd moved up was from interns, to attendings, to surgeons. He knew I was angling for a professional promotion. Had it been so long that he'd forgotten who he was dealing with?

My nostrils flared as my gaze narrowed on a spot between his chin and neck. I knew first hand how sensitive that spot was, and what I could get him to do if I bit down hard there. I watched his throat work and his eyes widen at the edges.

I let out a low exhale and gave him a nod. I hadn't forgotten what Wanda told me. I needed Rowe's vote if I wanted that promotion. So, instead of sassing him like I wanted to, like I knew he wanted me to, I put on my most jovial smile and turned to face the congregation.

"I would love to show you the good work we do here at Sacred Heart."

And I did just that. I took them to the ground floor and showed them where we did intake for new patients. I told them about the new system we'd put in to triage patients and keep track of them. As we made the rounds, many of the nurses' smiles were stiff; a few of the doctors' were, too. The patients stared at the women in habits.

The patients stared because it was not typical to see a nun in a habit nowadays, even though they'd once been a fixture in charitable hospitals. The doctors and nurses stared because they worried over what it would mean to mix religious doctrine with the care of their patients. Catholic health care followed ethical directives that put a bull's-eye on women's reproductive health.

As our tour of the ER was coming to a close, we came across a nurse trying to calm an irate patient.

"I'm sorry, sir," said the nurse. "But Medicare won't cover that."

"I've worked for forty years of my life." The patient's voice was gravely. His eyes were glassy, and he rubbed at his nose as he spoke. "I've paid the government at every pay check, and now you won't keep your end of the promise."

The nurse stood her ground. There was nothing much that she could do. We'd all been in her same position, and we had to take the same stance.

Beside me, I felt Sister Ruth tense. She stepped out of the congregation and approached the patient. Sister Mary Helena reached out to her, but her hand was beyond the younger woman's habit. Sister Ruth spoke quietly with the patient. His eyes lightened as he listened to her. Once she was finished speaking, Sister Ruth turned back to the nurse.

"The church will cover the cost of this man's bill," she said.

"God bless you," said the patient as he returned to the nurse.

When Sister Ruth rejoined us, she received a look of reproach from Sister Mary Helena. The men, however, puffed up their chests as though they'd done something, but not a single one of them had come out of their pockets to help. Sister Ruth caught my gaze.

"That man is a junkie," I said to her quietly. "He's been in here every week, and he'll be back."

Sister Ruth nodded slowly. "It's not my place to judge someone's failings, only to heal their injuries."

I couldn't resist. "All injuries?"

She turned those crystal blue eyes on me. They caught me up short for a second. They looked other-worldly, like she was an angel walking the earth.

"We had a woman in here with an ectopic preg-nancy a few days ago," I said. "She needed an emer-gency abortion or she would've died. Would we have been able to heal her injury under the church's judgment?"

Sister Ruth folded her hands in front of her habit. "Christ inspires all of his followers to meet the needs of the most vulnerable. We reveal God's love for all through compassionate service."

"Would you have let that woman die for your beliefs?"

Sister Ruth faced me. "My belief has nothing to do with it. My duty, as a child of God and as a nurse, is to ensure the best quality of life for my patients."

It wasn't exactly a yes, but neither was it exactly a no. I was even more intrigued at the fire in those blue depths. I wondered what lengths this woman would go to if she were pushed hard enough. I didn't have the chance to find out.

Sister Ruth bowed her head and joined the others. With the tour nearly over, I headed to the elevators to return them to the executive suite. But one elevator was down today and there was a line of people waiting including two patients on gurneys.

"We could take the stairs," I suggested. "It's only two flights."

The group followed me to the service stairwell. When I got to the door, I was pulled up short. There was high-pitched, feminine moaning bouncing off the walls of the stairwell. I looked through the glass pane and I saw a woman on her knees. The scrubs hanging off her ass told me she was a nurse. A thick, brown dick thrust in and out of her mouth.

I looked up at the clothed man's body. I knew the face I'd see there before my gaze met his chin.

"Nurse Cleo, let us pass," said Dr. Page.

I turned my back to the door, using my body to cover the glass pane that would allow them to see through. "Why don't we go back and wait for the elevator?"

I didn't know what I was thinking? Why didn't I let them see? That was Nurse Charity on her knees in the stairwell. This would certainly knock her out of the running for the promotion, leaving me to get exactly what I needed to take care of me and my family.

"The stairs will be quicker," said Page.

I hesitated for one second. When he reached around me, I stepped out of his way. As the door opened wider, Charity's voice carried up the stairwell.

"Give me that cock."

"I don't feel right about this, Nurse Charity," came Eagle's dispassionate voice. "What if we get caught?"

"Oh, I want to get caught," she said. "That turns me on. I'm a naughty, naughty, little nurse."

"I just wanted you to take care of my brother," said Eagle. His tone was surprisingly even for someone who was being jerked off. "We can't pay the bill."

"Oh baby, don't worry. When you stick that thick, cock in my tiny little pussy that is going to be my payment. I'm going to take care of both you and your brother."

One by one I heard each member of the congregation and hospital staff gasp. It was a sight. A large, black man with his cock shoved down the throat of a petite, white woman. But Eagle's hands were behind his back, grasping the bars of the staircase. Charity's hands were all over him and herself. She looked like she was taking total advantage of the poor man.

At the sound of the gasps, Charity scrambled up, which was difficult with her pants down around her ankles. She fell back, and her ass hit the cold concrete. Her knees fell open giving every one a clear view of that tiny, little pussy.

Above her, Eagle calmly tucked himself back inside his pants. His hazel eyes traveled up and found mine. And then he winked at me.

TEN

The nurse's station was still atwitter with Charity's lewd performance and quick dismissal. The nurses and doctors alike buzzed about how she took advantage of a patient's brother and had her way with the poor, helpless, cash-strapped man. There was talk of charges, but the patient and his family declined to press any.

I sat swiveling in my rolling chair. Eagle hadn't batted an eye when he'd seen the monetary charges accruing on Crow's bill. I'd expected him to pay in cash, but he handed over a black AMEX. He was no poor, helpless victim.

But he was strapped all right. In more ways than one.

The sight of his thick cock on Charity's tongue

had made my own mouth water. Part of me wanted to direct him to shove his dick down her throat until she choked on it. The other part of me wanted a taste for myself.

I didn't suck a lot of dick. Not as a rule. Not because I wasn't good at it. I just didn't meet a lot of guys whose dicks I had an interest in allowing inside my body. I much preferred to be the one dicking them. But Eagle's dick...

Unfortunately, it had been tainted with Charity's grime. My mind kept racing back to Eagle asking how he could repay me. Although Crow's bill was settled, Eagle continued to act as though he owed me something.

I knew sex was exactly what he'd had in mind as a payment plan. Had he tried to make the same deal with Charity? I didn't think so. When he'd pulled his dick out of her mouth, he'd winked at me. Had he gotten caught with her on purpose?

I'd told him the night before that that stairwell got a lot of traffic. He knew I wanted that promotion. He heard Page invite me on the tour. He knew that Charity was my competition. It all added up.

I bolted out of my seat and headed to his brother's room. There was only one person in the room; the patient. Crow's room had always been filled with people. It was the first time I'd seen him by himself without having to clear the room first.

Crow slept peacefully, he looked childlike in his unguarded sleep. He looked childlike when he was awake, too. It was just that when he was awake, he also looked like a little devil.

I swallowed my disappointment and got down to work. I checked his vitals, turning on the sound of the machines to make sure they were functioning. I pulled the clipboard from the bottom of his bed. The metal of the board clanged against the metal of the hospital bed. I went to his head and fluffed his pillows, then fluffed again. Finally, he stirred.

"Oh, did I wake you?" I said.

Crow's grin was lazy as it spread across his waking face. The man had a panty-melting smile. He wasn't aiming it purposefully at me. I had to assume that smile was just always loaded.

"I thought you were Mary Katherine," he mumbled in a bedroom voice. "I sent her home an hour ago to get some proper sleep. Do you know what?"

He crooked his finger for me to lean in. I couldn't help myself, his grin was infectious. I leaned in.

"I'm going to marry her." Crow's grin reminded me of a schoolboy with a new toy.

I grinned back. I knew there were some drugs in his system, but the thought of his fiancée made Crow's eyes go hazy. He shifted his head in the cocoon of over-fluffed pillows and turned to me. His eyes cleared and sharpened.

"Are you looking for Eagle?" he said. "Or are you hiding from him?"

I turned back to the machine, which showed his vital signs were strong. I made a show of adjusting the knobs. "I was checking on my patient."

"I heard the last nurse who did that got more than she bargained for," he chuckled. "I didn't like her. She pulled the covers too tight. I'm glad he got rid of her."

My hands fell away from the knobs and landed on the bars of his bed. "So, he did do it on purpose."

Crow blinked slowly. Intelligence beamed through the charm of his gaze. He didn't respond.

I inhaled and let out a gush of air. "I didn't ask him to do that."

Crow shrugged. "My brother can be intense when he latches onto something."

"Eagle hasn't latched onto me."

Crow closed his eyes and smiled. He didn't look

young now that he was awake and his eyes were pinched closed. He looked older than his age, and tired. He took a deep breath and blew it out.

"He blames himself for this." Crow swept his hand down his injured body.

"I thought it was an accident."

He shrugged again, opening his eyes. His focus was far off, likely back on the racetrack. "I had that curve. Then that jackass bumped me."

"How's that Eagle's fault?"

"Eagle and Roman, that's the other driver, they got into an argument before the race. Roman called E the N-word. Had some choice words for my other brothers, too. E thinks Roman took it out on me on the track."

I'd seen my fair share of brawls between men. They hurled creative insults at each other. They might use their fists. But cars? I shuddered at the thought. "Can't you report it?"

"The track ruled that it was an intentional bump."

"So that asshole's going to jail?"

"No, he's been fined and he'll sit out a race."

"That's bullshit." I forced the words out through gritted teeth. "I wish it was illegal to be a racist piece of shit." If it were, there would be a large number of people from my past in jail.

"It is, actually. Eagle's older brother is in the FBI Hate Crimes Division. He came down the other day to investigate." Crow looked up at me thoughtfully. "Eagle has a high sense of right and wrong and justice. His mom's a judge and his dad's a rocket scientist."

My mouth formed an O.

"E builds engines and races cars. The finish line is black and white with a set of sequential steps to get to it. He doesn't like to lose control. He's been feeling out of control since I hit that wall. He's looking for a distraction; something or someone he can tinker with and gain mastery over."

I felt a tingling in my long, underserved clit. I pressed my thighs together to temporarily quench that thirst. "He looks like the kind of guy who can get any girl he wants. I'm not interested."

"Don't let him know that," Crow grinned and closed his eyes. "E likes a challenge. He has the other girls figured out. You're a puzzle for him to solve. He'll become obsessed with making you come. Ellie says that's his love language."

I waited for Crow to say more, but all that came from him was a soft snore. I pulled the covers over his chest and then loosened them. I turned off the sound of the machines, straightened the clipboard at the edge of his bed, and quietly left the room.

My shift was nearly over. I would be heading home soon. On time for once. I gathered my things from my locker and headed to the exit. When I came through the glass doors, sitting outside lounging on a bench, was Eagle.

His gaze latched onto mine. Then it swept over my body. I felt heated every place his gaze landed. I pressed my thighs together again, but the friction only made it worse.

"You get what you wanted?" he asked.

"Probably," I said, sitting down beside him. I knew he was talking about the promotion. "It feels kind of hollow, though. I wanted to win it because I'm better than her."

"Victory doesn't always work that way. People cheat. Sometimes the bad guy pulls into the lead."

His eyes looked far away like Crow's had. I knew he was thinking about the race. I decided to distract him.

"How do you know I'm not a bad guy?"

His smile returned. Just an uptick at the corner of his mouth. "Oh, Nurse Cleo, I suspect you're a very, very bad girl."

He looked at me. Locked me in place with those hazel eyes. I stared back. He needed to know I wasn't some chit to be easily swayed.

"You ready to get off?" he asked.

I shifted my hips in the seat. Crow had said he'd be relentless in trying to get in my pants and make me come. Why was that a bad thing?

"You've been here all day," Eagle said. "You should be getting off soon."

"Yeah, my shift is over."

"Come on, I'll take you home."

My gaze snapped to his. My eyebrows narrowed into a low V at the directive.

The other side of his mouth kicked up. His head dipped along with his gaze and his tone. "May I escort you home, Nurse Cleo?"

The *may I* made my panties moist. I hesitated, pulling my arms across my chest and my bag in my lap. They were poor protections against this man. "I was going to call an Uber."

"You were going to let a stranger drive you home?"

"You're a stranger."

"No, I'm not," he said simply.

I dropped the bag and my arms and turned to

face him head on. "I'm not going to have sex with you. I'm taking a break from men."

Eagle nodded. Completely un-put off. "Lucky for you I got serviced this morning. I'll get you home safe."

There was command in his voice, but he was holding back. Still, that note of authority was a loaded weapon on his hip just waiting to be unholstered and cocked. If he kept pointing it at me I wouldn't be able to resist pointing my own loaded weapon at him.

"I saved your friend," I said. "You got me a promotion. Are we even now?"

"I didn't realize we were keeping score."

"I think we are. I'd rather not be in your debt. Seems dangerous."

He laughed. "It is."

"I want us to be even."

"No."

"Yes."

"Make me."

I inhaled. The air sizzled between us. My fingers shook, itching to reach for something to clamp his nipples with. "What are you doing? You're a Dom. I'm not a sub."

"I can see that."

"Then what are you doing? I'm not going to submit to you."

"Maybe I want to be friends."

Now, I laughed.

"And yes," he said, "I want to fuck you. Not because I want to break you or bend you to my will. Because it looks like you need a good fuck and that's what friends do for each other. At least in my world."

I stared at him, weighing my options, my desires, my needs. It was nice to do that, to not have to worry about another person's feelings for a moment.

"I'm going to let you take me home," I said. "But I'm not going to let you fuck me."

"Sounds fair."

He didn't say *for now*. But it was implied, loud and clear.

ELEVEN

The drive across town was in mostly silence. Eagle seemed to know that I craved a moment of peace. He even put on classical music. It wasn't my jam, but the haunting strings soothed me.

"Who is this?" I asked.

"That's my brother Hawk's baby sister."

"She's a violinist?"

"A cellist." He grinned with a fond look in his eyes. His big body relaxed into the driver's seat. "Gabby's been playing ever since she was a kid. The instrument is still bigger than her. She's good, yeah?"

The question didn't need an answer. The notes nearly lulled me into sleep. But then the sounds of a growling motor pulled me awake. I felt Eagle's tension before I opened my eyes.

Outside the car window four white guys in a dark car surrounded us. A bright swastika was painted on their hood. I recognized the driver as the one who'd walked out of the ER when Crow was wheeled in. Recognition didn't light his blue eyes. They narrowed in disgust as they took in both Eagle and me.

"Hey, black bird," shouted the man in the passenger seat. He had dark tattoos on his milky skin. The tattoos were mostly water colored; it was their content that was dark. "Too bad about last weekend's loss."

"It's not a loss when the opponent cheats," said Eagle.

Tattoo guy smirked. "Yeah, tell that shit to your little brother. Is little Tweety Bird okay?"

Eagle gripped the wheel. The blood drained from his fingertips as he held on. I wasn't sure if he was trying to hold on to his temper or if he was bracing himself for a fight.

"That's a fine piece of ass," said the driver. "I would've brought her out of the fields and into the big house back in the day. I know you and your brother's like to share your cunts. You share her?"

"Put your dick out and see," I said.

"Oh," the driver laughed. "I like her. A little

sapphire. I'll race you for her, Kunte. Winner gets to fuck her."

Before Eagle could open his mouth, I got there first. I leaned over Eagle and stuck my head out his driver's side window, addressing my comments to the Nazi with a fetish for dark meat. "I think you should take him up on his offer."

Eagle turned to me, clearly surprised. We were so close that the puffs of air coming from his nostrils kissed my cheek. I turned to look at him. Our lips were in alignment, but they didn't touch.

Racist pieces of shit catcalled out the window. Horns honked behind us to go. But time stopped as I looked down at Eagle's lush, bitable lips. I wasn't big on kissing, but I wanted his lips on me. And not necessarily on the lips affixed to my face.

"Come on," I smiled at Eagle, but my comments were still directed at the pale driver in the next lane. Pity dripping from my lips as I spoke. "It's the only way that pencil dick has a chance of getting fucked. Even if it's a small, tiny, slim, little chance."

Eagle's mouth quirked up. His tongue dipped out and he licked at the top of his lip. For a moment I forgot we weren't out in the middle of the street challenging assholes to a street race. Eagle gave me a light push aside, returning me to my seat. Then he turned and looked out the window, giving the other car and its driver a signal.

Eagle turned back to the road and gripped the steering wheel. In the other car, the driver winked at me. The passenger stuck his tongue out and flicked it around in a lewd gesture that did nothing for me. I pulled at my seat belt and braced my feet against the floorboards.

"You are as good as you say you are, right?" I whispered to Eagle. Even if he wasn't I had no doubt I could break that pencil dick if I got him behind closed doors. But I didn't want to test that theory.

The tension melted from Eagle's face. He grinned, as he looked me up and down. His assessing gaze did everything for me. "I like you, Cleo."

He turned his attention back to the road and revved the engine. I felt a thrill in my core. Eagle inhaled, like a bloodhound scenting fresh meat.

The light turned green. The other car pulled off into the night, in a plume of smoke and a screech of tires. My heart plummeted as we sat in park.

"Fucking amateur," Eagle chuckled as he put his car in gear.

"It looks like they're in the lead to me."

Eagle shook his head as he eased on the gas.

"They lost traction when they sped off like that. It's going to make for a slower acceleration."

I didn't understand anything but the red tail-lights in front of me. Was I going to have to go off with those guys tonight? Would Eagle stand by and let me be the payment for the debt? I had been the one to make the bet, not him. Fuck.

"Just give her a second," Eagle said. He caressed the steering wheel like it was the curve of a woman's hip. "She's about to reach her sweet spot and then she's going to explode."

How did he make everything sound sexual?

Beside me Eagle gave the car more gas. I watched the odometer tick up. The other car came closer. We were headlight to taillight. I could see the other driver looking down at his odometer. His body motion looked as though he was stomping on the gas, but the car's speed did not increase.

Eagle shifted the gears of his car and gave it more gas. When he did, we took off. It felt like we were flying.

We pulled in front of the jerks, and then with another shift, we took off. Their headlights receding into the night. Before they were completely out of sight, I turned in my seat and stuck both middle fingers up for them to see through the rearview window of Eagle's car. I may have also hurled a few choice curse words and lewd phrases at them as we sped down the street.

When I turned and sat back down, Eagle chuckled. "I really like you, Cleo."

TWELVE

We pulled up to my house doing the speed limit. We parked on the street and Eagle stepped out of the car. Before I got my seatbelt off, he'd opened the passenger side door.

"I can open my own door," I said.

He shrugged. "Blame my mother. She's a feminist, but she screwed up and raised a gentleman."

I ignored his offered hand and stepped out of his car on my own. Eagle chuckled as he shut the door. He fell in step beside me and we rounded my car. There was another citation on the window. I cursed. So did Eagle.

"Accident?" he asked.

"No," I sighed. "Purposeful."

"It looks like you ran into another car."

"Yup."

He doubled over with laughter. When he straightened he said, "I really, really like you, Cleo."

His eyes roamed my body and I heated. I was going to have to destroy these panties. First that race where every time he'd increased his speed it made the blood race through my skin, and then settle in my core. It was boiling now that those hazel eyes stared into mine. And he seemed to know I was suffering.

"Let me fix it," he crooned.

"No."

"Fine, let's make a deal."

"I'm not trading sexual favors with you."

"I was going to give you a low quote for my mechanical services. My body doesn't come cheap."

I grit my teeth, but a giggle stole through. This man kept catching me off guard. I needed to get away from him. Or on top of him. I couldn't decide which idea was best.

"Cleo?"

I turned to the front door. Toy stood at the top of the stairs. Her eyes locked on Eagle. I heard her breath catch as she took him in. Then her gaze and her head lowered submissively.

I rolled my eyes. She was such a slut. It had been

a long time since I'd invited someone home to play with her. She obviously thought she was getting a treat tonight.

Eagle's gaze latched onto Toy as he spoke to me. "Invite me in."

He sounded like a vampire scenting easy prey. It was as though Toy's bowed head was her bared neck cranked back as an offering. My neck cranked around for an entirely different reason. I didn't take well to men telling me what to do, especially when it came to my playthings.

Eagle turned those hazel eyes back to me. His gaze swept over my pinched expression. His lips quirked and he lowered his head and his gaze. "Please," he said.

Oh, he was good. He was really good.

He peaked up at me from beneath thick lashes. A demon in a wolf's coat. I turned on my heel and preceded him up the stairs. Toy stepped behind the door. Her breath came in excited pants as Eagle and I crossed the threshold.

"Victoria."

"Yes, Mistress."

"This is my... friend, Eagle."

Eagle grinned at the word before turning his attention to my toy. His gaze raked over her and then he turned back to me. I realized what he was doing and it made me wetter. I gave a slight incline of my head, giving him permission to approach her.

"It's nice to meet you, Victoria."

Toy's gasp was audible. Her eyes stayed down. Her throat worked as she tried to swallow her excitement.

"Can I get you something to drink?" I asked Eagle.

"You got a beer?"

"I'll get it." Toy bounced on her toes and raced into the kitchen.

We followed her down the hall. By the time we got into our small kitchen, Toy had pulled out two beers and was looking in the drawer for the bottle opener.

Eagle went to the sink. He turned on the faucet and aimed his hands at the stream. But he halted, staring down into the sink. There was a bucket in the basin. Inside the bucket weren't dishes.

Toy had been cleansing our arsenal of sex toys.

Her gaze went to me. Her eyes widened, unsure if a punishment was forthcoming. Then her gaze narrowed, as though she were contemplating if she'd prefer it. My gaze was locked on Eagle as he considered the array of toys in the sink.

"You know," said Eagle, turning off the faucet and drying his hands on a dishtowel. "When I was a kid, I used to make pocket pussies out of hand towels." He turned from the sink filled with vibrators, butt plugs, and nipple clamps and grabbed his opened beer.

I wrapped my thumb and index finger around the neck of my bottle and took a swig. "How did that work?"

"Grab me the dish towel," he said to Toy.

She did, reaching for the damp towel with trembling hands. She came and stood before Eagle. Her hands were outstretched with the item, her gaze fixed on his chest.

"Do you guys have plastic gloves?"

I nodded my head towards the cabinet below the sink. Toy obediently went to fetch the other item.

"Let me use your hair tie." Eagle reached behind Toy and grabbed her ponytail. He gave the band holding her hair together a rough yank. She gasped, her eyes closing in ecstasy. Eagle smiled at her before turning back to me.

"First with the towel," he said. "Can you put your fingers in there, Toy. Hold the glove. Yes, that's a good girl."

Eagle rolled the folded towel around Toy's

fingers and the glove. Once he had a cylindrical shape, he slid the towel off of Toy's fingers, leaving the glove inside. He wrapped bands around both edges of the tubular contraption.

"Then you stretch the end of the glove over the towel." He did so, flipping the elastic band over the edge. "Add some lube, and jack off." He made a jerking motion with the towel-pussy to demonstrate.

"Nice," I grinned. "I used cucumbers and bananas. Once an eggplant."

His eyebrows rose with respect at the mention of the eggplant. "You're making me hungry."

"Did you know they used to use goat eyelids as cock rings?" I asked.

"That's some sick shit," he grimaced.

"I preferred the good old electric toothbrush, electric razor, and a good old cell phone to get off."

He nodded. "My favorite was the vacuum cleaner."

"What?" I choked on my beer.

"That suction?" Eagle said in a dreamy tone. "Yeah, that Dyson is an equal opportunity pleaser. You never tried it?"

I shook my head no, still unable to fathom how one might use a vacuum cleaner on their genitals without getting seriously injured.

"You guys got a vacuum?" he asked.

I nodded. I turned to Toy, but she was already in motion, headed to the hall closet. She brought back our vacuum and set it before Eagle.

"Thank you, sweetheart." He pulled out the cord and plugged the vacuum into a nearby outlet. "May I?"

Eagle's gaze locked on mine. His lashes were low but the light of mischief burned bright in those hooded eyes. He was trying to break down my barriers, and he was doing a good job. I pulled a wall of protection between us.

"Toy, get undressed for our guest."

"Yes, Mistress."

I knew she was eager, but she kept her eyes down. Her chest panted as she pulled off the few articles of clothing that she wore. She came to stand bare before him.

Eagle lifted her up and onto the dining table. He went to part her knees, but they flopped open before his fingertips made it within an inch of her. He chuckled and then stomped on the ON switch for the vacuum. Toy jerked as the device came to life.

Eagle pulled off the rectangular attachment, the only one we ever used to clean the floor. "I used to use it without any attachment. I've never felt suction like this from anyone's mouth. I'd blow in under a minute every time."

That's because he hadn't met me. But I wasn't going to suck him off. I was simply watching this little demonstration purely for educational purposes.

In place of the rectangular attachment, Eagle affixed the long, flat suction attachment that looked like it was suited to go between the couch cushions. Toy let out a keening moan as he twisted the device on.

He ran it up her inner thighs. I watched as the long nozzle pinched and sucked her skin in, turning it pink with hickies. "How's that feel, little toy?"

"Good, sir."

He moved the device to the crease at her right hip, just on the other side of her labia. Toy's skin was nude, just the way I liked her. So there was no hair getting caught up in the suction, just her flesh. Eagle moved the nozzle lightly over her skin. I could see her flesh arch up towards the sucking lips of the nozzle.

When the lips of the nozzle landed on her left labia, Toy's knees bounced up and down and she grit her teeth trying to stay in place. Her knuckles drained of blood as they gripped the edges of the table.

Slowly, the lips of the nozzle marched their way up to her clit. Along the way, they sucked in her labia. Her flesh rose to meet the flat attachment, but Eagle held it just far enough that her skin didn't get sucked in. For her part, Toy arched up trying to get caught.

I watched Toy fight the losing battle. Just as her body arched and moved with his movements, so too did my eyes. Without warning, Eagle launched his final strike. He swooped in and landed that nozzle directly on her clit.

Toy's eyes opened wide. Her head arched back. Her hips came off the table and her knees fluttered like a bird trying to take off from the ground.

I watched her, trembling helplessly as he held her down and held the attachment over her clit. She came and came and came. Tears streamed down her cheeks. Desperate whimpers came from her raw throat.

I knew I should step in, but I was too fascinated. I'd never seen an orgasm last this long. I was curious to see how much longer he could make her go.

But then he pulled the suction off her. Toy collapsed down onto the table. She shut her legs and rolled to her side. Her body trembled. She barely made a sound. The only thing that filled the air was the sound of the vacuum sucking down empty air.

Eagle stepped on the ON switch again, turning the device off. "That's why it's my favorite. Little effort, maximum results."

My response was non-intelligible. It didn't matter. Eagle's focus was on Toy.

"You okay, little toy?"

Toy's response was no better than mine. Her eyes were closed and her breathing ragged.

"I'll put her to bed." He scooped her up in his arms. Then he turned to me, with my toy against his chest, and stared.

It took me a full minute before I understood what he needed. Directions. I stood on wobbly legs and led him upstairs to Toy's room.

She was comatose as he laid her in the bed and pulled the covers over her. I stood in the doorway and watched. By the time he'd straightened I'd made up my mind.

I was going to fuck this man. I was going to tie him up and make him beg. I was going to bring him to his knees and make him mine.

"Thank you for letting me play with your toy," he said as I closed Toy's door. "I needed that distraction."

"You could have asked her for a blow job before you made her comatose."

"I have manners," he said. "You don't jack off in someone's sub without asking."

We stood at the top of the stairs. He faced me and leaned against the wall. I saw in his eye that he was waiting for me to say something. He knew I was aroused. I know he could smell how wet my panties were.

"Do you need to be taken care of?" I asked.

He shrugged. "There's a party at my house tonight. We're celebrating that Crow's going to be okay. I'll have someone take care of me there."

Again, we stood staring at each other. I knew that all I had to do was give him a word and I could have him. I knew it would be magnificent.

But not tonight.

Eagle was a tricky one. If I wasn't careful, I might trip up. And then he'd have me instead of the other way around. This was war and I had to take time and prepare for the next battle because clearly he'd won a few today while I was just coming to realize I was under attack.

So, instead of dropping my panties, or making him drop his pants, I walked him to the door. I opened the door and he stepped across the threshold without protest. When I looked in the driveway towards his car, I saw that mine was gone.

"Relax," he said and eased a hand on my tensed shoulder. "Hawk came by to pick it up twenty minutes ago."

"You stole my car?"

"No," he said. "I did not steal your car. I'm fixing it. I'll have it good as new in two days."

I saw red. He'd already won one battle on my home turf. He'd begun a second and I hadn't even noticed. Even worse, he was fighting dirty, using the nastiest tactic in any man's arsenal; chivalry.

"You're an asshole," I said.

"You're welcome." He grinned. "I'll pick you up in the morning for work."

"You're trying to make me dependent on you." I shoved a finger into his chest. It did nothing to move him.

"I'm fixing your car." He caught my hand, and rubbed his thumb over my wrist. "Pay whatever, however, and whenever you want. Or not at all. It's your choice."

"How'd you even get it started?"

He snorted at that.

I yanked my hand out of his grasp. "What if I call the cops and report my car missing?"

He reached into his pocket and pulled out his wallet. "Here's how to find me."

He handed me a card with Watchers Crew written on it overtop a logo of winged tires. Below the logo was an address and phone number.

Eagle winked and then headed up the drive. Before I could think of any insults to hurl at him, he was gone in a squeal of tires, leaving his mark on the asphalt of my driveway.

THIRTEEN

He just watched me. We sat across from each other while Toy writhed in orgasm. Her nipples were straining pinpoints as she arched her back. Her heels dug into the carpet and she ground her ass down as her pussy juices dripped into the fibers. Her arms and thighs shook from the impact. It was a beautiful sight, but he wasn't looking at her. Eagle was watching me.

He rose from his chair. He walked around Toy as her orgasm continued to wrack her body. He came before me, bent his knees, and sank down to my feet. His head was lowered but his eyes were lifted.

"May I?"

I spread my thighs for him. He didn't touch. He just looked.

His slow inhales and languid exhales lulled me into a meditative state. His face contorted in reverence like my pussy was an altar and he worshiped before me. He just looked and breathed. Nothing more.

After long moments of meditation, he hummed a sigh that sounded like a long *Om* or *Amen*. With that single utterance, the floodgates deep inside me opened and I came. I came so hard it woke me up.

My eyes slammed open and I moaned. I was really coming -hard. I pressed my thighs together, and still I came. I put my hands between my legs and rolled into a fetal position, and still I came.

I'd never had a wet dream before. I'd never come from a dream before. I'd never come at the thought of a man before.

Lying wide-awake in my bed, with my body still trembling from the impact of the dream fuck, I found myself still horny. For the first time in a long time, I wanted a cock in me; an actual cock. A long, thick, Hershey brown cock with a pink tip that wept a clear dollop of goodness.

I sat up in the bed and winced. My pussy throbbed as though I'd had a good bout of rough sex. I stretched my body like a cat and slid out of bed.

I dressed for work and then slipped out of my

room. Peaking in Toy's room, I saw that she still slept. He'd worked her over good. I expected I would need to buy new vacuum cleaner attachments soon.

At the front door, the mail slot opened to reveal a sliver of bright sun. A selection of colored envelopes and one package hit the floor with the thud. I grabbed for the package. The from label's address showed the online sex shop that I favored.

I opened the package and pulled out a cock ring. It had been for Dr. West, but he no longer deserved such a privilege. I twirled the ring around my finger dreaming up all the ways I would break Eagle in the coming days.

An orange envelope that lay in the pile of white mail caught my eye. I knew the pile of white envelopes on the floor were bills. I opened the orange envelope and pulled out an eviction notice.

That bitch.

For the first time in her life Lisa had kept her word. Well, it didn't matter any longer. I'd have the money in my next paycheck now that the promotion was all but guaranteed to be mine.

I picked up all the envelopes, including the offensive orange one, and shoved them in a drawer. I turned and looked around the house. The paint was peeling off the ceiling. We really needed to get a carpet cleaning, or a brand new carpet. I could hear the heater straining. The AC had been on the fritz and it probably wouldn't last another season. Why the hell was I working so hard for this damned house?

Because this was where Toy felt safe. She hadn't been outside, not even in the backyard, in two years. We couldn't move. We were going to stay here where she felt safe. I'd just put some of my raise into the house and fix it up nice.

Speaking of raises and new jobs, I looked at the clock. I needed to be to work soon.

Outside, the driveway was empty. Eagle had promised to take me to work after he'd taken my car away last night. But where was he? Then a thought hit me. What if he didn't show?

The moment the thought entered my mind; I heard the growl of a motor coming down the street. I looked back out the window, and there he was. He was dressed all in black; black jeans that hugged his powerful legs; a black T-shirt; and a black leather, motorcycle jacket that looked expensive. Black shades covered his face. He was pulling off a black helmet by the time I closed and locked the door behind me.

Eagle leaned against his bike and grinned at me.

I leaned against the doorframe and grinned back. It was a power play. Who was going to budge first? Who would come to whom?

He was far away but I saw the chuckle and lift of his shoulders. He shoved off his bike and came toward me. I shoved off the frame and came down the steps.

"Sleep well?" he asked.

"Yeah. You?"

"You were in my dreams. You ruined my new sheets."

I licked my lips, but I kept my mouth shut. I didn't tell him what he'd done to my sheets.

Eagle pulled something from his back pocket, but didn't show it to me. "I brought you something."

"I have something for you, too." My clit tingled with excitement as I looked up at the corner of his mouth. I knew I'd get to nuzzle along the seam of those lips soon. "But I'm not going to give it to you yet."

"Will you tell me what I'm waiting for?"

I took his free hand and put it between my thighs.

Eagle nodded slowly as he cupped my pussy. "Just what I wanted. How did you know? My present for you is ready now."

He opened his free hand and produced a box of Ben Wa balls. He presented them to me with a grin. In my hand, I still held the cock ring.

"I tell you what," I said. "I'll take your balls, if you wear my ring."

"Deal." Eagle reached down and unzipped his pants.

I looked out at the driveway. It was eight in the morning. People were preparing to leave for work. School kids were boarding a bus.

Eagle pulled out his dick and slid the ring down its long length. Once it was seated at the base of his cock, he hefted himself back in his pants and zipped himself in. The doors to the yellow bus closed and pulled away with none of the youth the wiser.

"You pervert," I said.

"You surprised?" He held the balls out to me in the palm of his hand. His eyes challenged me.

My scrub pants were the kind with a drawstring. I loosened the string. I took one ball and slid it inside. It was a heavy weight. He held the second ball out. I tried to hide my gulp, but he caught it. I slid the second one inside.

Eagle smiled. "It's going to be a long day."

We both walked up the driveway with slow, careful steps.

He held out a hand to help me climb on the bike. I had to clench to keep the balls in as I raised my leg. Oh my Kegels would be sweating today.

Eagle handed me a helmet. Then he raised his leg and slid onto the bike. I didn't miss his wince as he adjusted himself on the seat in front of me.

"I didn't take you for a motorcycle kind of guy."

"I like all engines," he said. "My brother's in town. He's the bike head. I was out with him after I dropped you off last night. I didn't think you'd mind the bike."

"I don't," I said wrapping my hands around his waist and clenching my thighs around his ass. "How many brothers do you have?"

"Prince is my actual blood brother. Hawk, Crow, and Owl are the brothers I chose."

"You don't like your blood brother?"

"I love my brother. We get along. No family traumas. But he doesn't live here, and he doesn't visit a lot. He says it's 'cause of his job, but I think it's because of a girl. Anyway, when he's here, we ride."

He started up the bike. The engine vibrated the balls deep inside me. I felt his ass tense. We both took a deep inhale as we adjusted our bodies and our minds to accommodate the devices interacting with our groins.

"Hold on tight," he chuckled.

He went from zero to sixty in less than five seconds. The vibrations from the seat dinged the balls inside me, and then they dinged each other. I felt like one of those grandfather clocks at noon. But the two hands of the clock stayed at noon for twenty minutes and the gonging didn't cease.

I could do nothing but hold onto Eagle for dear life as we sped down the highway. My heart was racing and my pussy was watering. It was the most exhilarating feeling of my life.

By the time we arrived at the hospital, my legs were jelly and my cunt was over-sensitized. A strong wind would've given me an orgasm. Eagle had to lift me off the bike. When my feet hit the ground, I wobbled.

"You good?" he asked.

"Never."

He chuckled.

"You?" I asked.

The devil would be jealous of the grin Eagle gave me. His hand trailed down my side. Then lower to my hip. I thought he'd go forward to my aching cunt, but instead his hand went to rest just above my ass. His gazed stayed glued to mine, his eyes asking permission. Before I could decide whether I was about to give it or not, my pager went off.

Eagle withdrew his hand and chuckled softly. That light breeze of his breath nearly broke me. "I'll come play with you later, Nurse Cleo."

FOURTEEN

Wanda was still out with the flu. That meant all the grunt work of management was thrust upon me. Top that off with the fact that we were a nurse down thanks to Charity. Her little performance brought the rest of the nursing staff to their knees as we were stretched thin with car accidents, a construction site injury, and one heart attack.

Amidst the chaos, I kept my cool. We all did. We were trained nurses used to pulling more than our fair share and then having a bit more piled on.

I was stuck behind a desk from morning to lunch, filling out paperwork, answering phones, triaging from behind a computer instead of out on the floor. I didn't get to see a patient for the first three hours of my shift.

None of it bothered me. I felt an overwhelming sense of fullness deep inside. I squeezed my thighs together and felt the Ben Wa balls inside me shift ever so slightly.

Most women went to the gym eager to keep their bellies flat or their thighs from getting thunderous. I was a proponent of working out, but it wasn't the exterior that I wanted to keep tight and right. I used Ben Wa balls on the regular to maintain my pelvic floor.

These ones that Eagle had gifted me were heavy, but they weren't a great challenge. I carried around heavier ones for long periods of time. The heaviness inside me was a constant reminder of the balls' owner.

I'd had them inside all morning and their weight in my groin was now making me feel as though I'd been fucked hard and long from behind. That kind of fuck where you don't come, and you kinda don't want to come any time soon because those deep thrusts with a thick cock that stretches you wide is just too damned good. So good, you spread your legs wider, arch your back more, toot your ass up higher, and cross your fingers that he's not close either because you want him to go just a little longer, a little harder.

By lunchtime, my channel was begging for a release. I headed out to the cafeteria to refuel my body. I'd stopped by Crow's room before heading down. The man was sleeping peacefully without any visitors. I hadn't seen Eagle since he'd dropped me off.

Even though my pussy ached I wouldn't be the first to cry uncle. I knew he was somewhere suffering with my ring around his cock. If he could take the torture, I would too. I paid for my chicken salad and turned to find a seat. And that's when I felt the buzzing in my panties.

There are cases of spontaneous orgasm. I know; I'd read up on all of them. It was known as Persistent Genital Arousal Disorder or PGAD — although I swore that using the term *disorder* was a misclassification. PGAD was a constant or spontaneous uncontrollable engorgement of the genitals, without any sexual desire, that could lead to persistent orgasms. It was a condition I wanted desperately. And it seemed like I was finally getting my wish.

I felt my vaginal lips swelling. Juices collected in my channel, and my walls lost their grip on the Ben Wa balls. I stopped walking and clenched my thighs together. With the friction of my inner thighs pressing together, my clit, which was nestled inside that fleshy heat, began to vibrate. I gulped down a deep breath of air and nearly dropped my salad.

I was about to come in the middle of the cafeteria, surrounded by doctors, nurses, staff, and patients. I looked up, desperate for the nearest exit. And then I saw him.

Eagle.

He leaned against a wall. His grin was wider than a hyena's scenting easy prey. He had a black gadget in his hand. There were buttons and a dial. It looked like a remote control.

Fuck me. The Ben Wa balls were a vibrator. And he had a remote. Fuck. Me.

"Cleo."

I turned to see Chief Rowe make his way toward me. Eagle was to my left. The crowded tables were to my right. The chief was approaching. My back was against the wall. There was no escape.

"I wanted to talk with you, Cleo," said the chief.

I cocked my head and glared at him.

His confident steps stuttered when he caught my gaze. He swallowed and his eyes lowered. He cleared his throat, and began again. Properly this time.

"I wanted to talk to you, *Nurse* Cleo."

Good boy. My puppies never forgot their tricks, or who owned them.

Chief Rowe went on to tell me about some minutia of management that any nurse could've dealt with. I only heard Charlie Brown's teacher squawking in my ear. The buzzing of the balls took my sense of hearing, taste, touch, smell, and time away.

I leaned my back against the wall. I glanced over to the left at the grinning man holding my dignity in the palm of his hands. Eagle was going to pay. Oh, he was going to pay good and plenty.

I shot him daggers, but the hell if I would yell uncle. I had absolute control over my orgasms. But damn, it had been so long. I knew that when I broke it was going to be big, and beautiful, and long, and loud.

And soon.

A hand settled at my forearm. It was as though the needle had scratched while playing my favorite tune just when it was getting to the best part of the song. I glared up at Chief Row who was trying to cut in on my jam.

"When you get this promotion," he said, "we'll be working more closely together again."

"That'll be great. It'll give me a chance to finally

meet your new wife. I'm sure we'll have lots to talk about."

Chief Rowe jerked his hand back. He babbled something else and took off in the other direction. I watched him walk away and noted that the record player in my panties had stopped humming any tune. Turning back to my left, I saw that Eagle was gone.

I turned out of the cafeteria and took the elevator to Crow's room. Once there, I stood in the open doorway to see that the patient still slept peacefully in the hospital bed, alone.

The door closed behind me. I turned and shoved Eagle's large body into the door. His face widened in surprise at my strength. It was a delighted surprise.

I reached down into his pants and grabbed his cock. Putting it in a five-fingered vise, I began to stroke. I massaged him with my palm and rubbed the head of his cock with my thumb. I had to use two hands. Eagle was a big boy.

His head slammed back into the door. He shut his eyes and uttered a curse. I worked him up good and fast. A weaker man would've already been on his knees. Not this man. But still, I knew the machinations of my hands and the restriction of the cock ring was driving him to the brink.

"You want your balls back?" I purred.

Eagle groaned and thrust into my eager hands. His face broke into a pleasure-slaked grin. Then he chuckled. I felt his hand move beside my hip, and then I heard a click.

The vibrations began again inside me. I had to assume he turned the device up to the highest setting. I let go of his cock and sank to my knees, which placed my face right at his groin.

Above me, he caught his breath. The vibrator dulled down to its lowest setting, which was still a lot.

"I can do this all day," he said. "You have a safe word?"

"No." I regained my footing and came to stand toe to toe with him. "Do you?"

"Yeah," he grinned. "It's *doctor*."

"Fuck you." Damn, I liked this guy.

"I know you get off on being watched, E." The voice came from the patient in the bed. Crow was grinning at us with his eyes closed and an arm tossed over his forehead. "But I need to rest, nurse's orders."

I turned back to Eagle. His eyes stared so hard at me I felt like he was licking me up like I was a dripping popsicle. I bit my lip like he was the chicken salad I'd lost on my way here.

"I get off at five," I said.

Eagle shook his head. "You're gonna get off sooner than that."

"Aw, but you won't." I patted his locked down cock.

"You are so much fun." Eagle laughed. "May I come over to your house and play tonight, Nurse Cleo?"

I had to take a deep breath before I answered. Every instinct in me wanted to shove this man to the floor and have him lick up the mess he'd made inside my panties. But I was a professional. The patient in the bed needed his rest and I had work today.

So, I nodded. I reached up into my pussy and pulled out his balls. He reached down into his pants and presented me with a ring.

We both palmed the toys in our hands while we grinned at each other like school children. Then I pulled open the door and went out. I would have him on his knees before the sun set.

FIFTEEN

When Eagle and I pulled up to the house, Toy was at the top of the steps. She bounced on her feet, like an eager puppy as Eagle approached her. It was the farthest she'd come out of the house in years.

"I hope you've been a good girl," Eagle said holding his palm out to her as he climbed the porch steps slowly.

Toy was just inside the threshold. Her eyes flicked from his outstretched hand to the space just across the threshold. Her bare toes were right at the edge. I watched her chest heave as she lifted her hand. Her fingers stretched, but they didn't reach his.

Eagle didn't pick up his pace, but Toy picked up her heel. I froze in place as she put one foot out the door and across the doorstep. Just that one step was enough to put her in his grasp.

Eagle took the last step. He pressed his body against hers and urged her back in the house. "Good girl."

Toy's chest heaved as though she'd run for her life. In a sense she had. Just that one step was farther than she'd allowed herself to go in years.

"Because if you've been a good girl," Eagle said, "your Mistress might let me play with you."

He turned and looked over his shoulder at me. His grin hitched up at the corner of his mouth. Suddenly, my chest was heaving. I was breathing hard like I was running for my life. I took the steps two at a time until I was inside the house and standing before the two of them.

"I've been good, Mistress," Toy said, her eyes fastened to the floor.

Toy's posture was one of submission. Her head was down, her shoulders forward, her hands at her sides.

Eagle's posture was one of invitation. His head was high, his gaze fixed on me. He still had his hands on Toy. I needed this man on his knees in a bad way.

I shut the door and turned the lock. "Undress him for me. But don't touch anything fun."

"Yes, ma'am."

I walked into the living room, shedding my own clothing as I went. Near the fireplace was a chest with a broken padlock. I flipped the lid and beheld my stockpile of treasures. Dildos of various sizes, colors and textures. An assortment of butt plugs, beads, and cock rings. There were nipple clips, clamps, and clothespins. And lube. Lots and lots of lube.

I turned and found Toy on her knees. Eagle's thick, erect dick bobbed in front of her as she slipped his pants down and off his bare feet. Eagle's gaze was on me as I laid out my toys.

"Aren't you going to ask what I'm about to do to you?" I straightened with my selection, holding it behind my back.

Eagle stood in the center of my living room; naked as the day he came into this world. His hand ran absently through Toy's hair as she remained on her knees perilously close to his bobbing dick.

"I think you've figured out I'm just as perverted as you," he said.

"No one's as perverted as me."

"It doesn't matter what you do to me, as long as it pleases you."

My fingertips tingled. Moisture pooled in my

palms. My nails itched. Eagle smiled as I came to his side. He kept his face forward as I rounded to his back. His high, rounded ass looked like marble. I had to take a deep breath before I took a whack at it.

His ass cheeks clenched. Down below, his toes curled in the carpet fibers. A low rumble of pleasure rolled through his chest and vibrated in his throat.

"Legs apart."

He complied, parting those powerful thighs.

"Keep them that way."

"Yes, ma'am."

I inhaled, feeling my heart pound in my throat. The paddle shook as my fingers trembled. I nearly dropped the device since my palms were so slippery. Out of the corner of my eye, I saw Eagle's grin kick up.

"You are not to come without my permission."

"Yes, ma'am."

"Down on your knees."

His jaw tensed, and for the first time he hesitated. His resistance excited me. I felt my nostrils flaring. I pulled my lip in my mouth as I watched the tension cross and leave his face. He sank down to the floor, on his knees. His face was right in line with my crotch. Any tension fled as that cocksure grin spread at the V of my pussy.

"Sniff," I said.

"Yes, ma'am." He drew the two syllables out with reverence. His nose came within millimeters of my crotch and he inhaled, good and long. My knees quaked as his breath dragged like a car cruising down a country lane.

After his inhale, he tilted his head up and peered into my eyes. I opened my mouth to tell him to cast his eyes down, only to discover I liked him watching me.

Anticipation flooded his dark eyes. Eagerness sparkled in the irises. Challenge dilated his pupils. He blinked, and patience reset his features.

What the holy fuck?

I marched back to my toy box and pulled out my flogger. When I turned, I expected him to protest. His gaze wasn't on the toy in my hand. It was locked on my eyes.

I marched over to him, twirling the handle in my palm. The leather straps made a whirling sound. Still kneeling beside him, Toy's chest rose and fell rapidly. Eagle only smiled up at me.

He tilted his head up, baring his neck, one of the most vulnerable parts of his body. The tip of his dick leaked excitement on the carpet. I aimed the straps there.

"Fuck," he hissed. His head fell back, his gaze hooded.

The straps made light contact with his dick, but enough to sting. The head of his dick reared up. His balls tightened. My inner muscles clenched around an empty channel. The hollowness whispered up along my clit and I had to take a deep gulp.

Although his head dipped back, his gaze never left mine. He straightened his body and rolled his neck. "Thank you, ma'am."

I narrowed my gaze at him. What the hell was this guy? He smelled like a Dom. Right now he looked like a pain slut.

Over in the corner, Toy whimpered as she eyed the swinging straps. I knew she was soaking her panties at the sound the flogger made as it whirred.

Eagle's eyes weren't on the flogger. They were on me.

I struck him again. This time on his chest. Again, he gasped and his gaze hooded, but his eyes didn't close. They stayed on me.

I struck his ass. His side. His back. I was striking him hard enough to leave marks now. And still, he would only gasp and dip his gaze. But right away, his gaze came back to me.

The excitement still danced in his eyes. They

would dip and nearly close. He would open his mouth and moan. But he didn't come.

I knew for a fact that what I was doing to him felt good. He should have blown by now. He wasn't impotent. His cock was hard and straining. But he didn't come. Neither did he offer a single complaint.

Okay, so not a pain slut. Not a switch either, since he clearly wasn't getting off with me forcing him to submit to his knees. And the orgasm denial wasn't making him sweat. Still, the sight of him in that posture had pushed me to my edge. I needed relief and soon.

I reached for a chair and sat. The cool wood was immediately slippery as my juices leaked out. Eagle's nostrils flared.

That was curious.

I spread my legs so that my pussy faced him. His throat worked as he swallowed. His pupils flitted here and there, from my face to my pussy. When he focused on my pussy, he took it all in as though my cunt was a lush forest he wanted to go hiking through.

I parted my labia, running two fingers along each side until my clit poked through. Eagle's dick bobbed rhythmically as I rubbed myself. His breathing shallowed and his gaze traveled back to my face. When his eyes traveled back to my face, his lips parted in wonder as they fixed on my mouth, my eyes, my nose.

That was interesting.

That was fascinating.

I worked myself up, sticking one, then two fingers inside myself and pumping.

"Fuck," he whispered. It was half a groan, half a plea.

I fingered my clit, rubbing round and round in light circles. I was having trouble keeping my own eyes open as the tension inside me pushed against my breaking point.

Eagle's breathing increased as he watched me. His eyes stayed focused on my face as his hips rocked, following my motion as though he were the one fucking me. Was he imagining thrusting his dick down my throat? Was that his kink? If so, why wasn't he touching himself?

With my free hand, I crooked a finger at him. He crawled over to me on his knees. I expected him to rise and come at me with his dick in hand.

But he didn't touch himself. His gaze never left my face. He was more interested in watching my pleasure than receiving any of his own. It seemed like an oxymoron; a man who got off on a woman's orgasm. And then I realized what he was, but it was too late.

I was coming, hard. My channel clenched around my fingers. My body doubled over as the orgasm washed through me, ringing me out after the long drought.

It took a long while for my body to come down. When I regained mastery over my limbs, I lifted my gaze to his.

"Fuck me," I growled.

"I'd be happy to." His hands came to my thighs, but I shoved him back.

"You're a fucking Service Top," I accused. "Aren't you?"

SIXTEEN

When I was a kid, I didn't read storybooks with princes and princesses. I wasn't one for fairytales or love stories. I loved horror stories and thrillers where the villains were the true heroes and heroines. It took a lot of personality to fuck with people's minds and mess them up inside and out.

I wasn't so warped that I wanted to make people crazy in the asylum sense. I liked to see how far I could bend them to my will. Could I make them eat out of my hand (or ass)? And if they were misogynist assholes or queen bitches, then yeah, I might break their spirit, but only to remake them in a better image.

What I did was a service to the world if you truly thought about it. I took villains and beat the pitbull out of them. I remade them into puppies on my leash.

But a Service Top? That was an animal I didn't know how to handle. It was a unicorn; something straight out of a storybook that you hear about, wish existed, but know something so magical, so fantastical, couldn't possibly be real.

But here one knelt before me; his stiff horn pointing up at me waiting to dispense its magic.

"Are you a Service Top?" I demanded.

Eagle tilted his head up. His posture looked submissive, but I wasn't deceived. He was placating me; giving me what he thought I wanted to please me. Allowing his body to be in service to me with the end goal of getting me off.

Fuck.

"I'm whatever you need me to be," he said.

Double fuck.

For the first time in my life I stood naked before a kneeling man and I didn't know what to do. He would let me do anything to him, as long as it got me off. For most women, hell for every single woman on the planet, that wouldn't be a bad thing. But for someone like me, someone who needed to be in control of the situation, it was a horror movie.

I needed the control. I craved it. I'd never let any

man or woman get the upper hand on me, and I wouldn't be starting now.

"Toy, come here."

Victoria hopped up and all but sprinted over to us. It was only a few steps but she was panting when she arrived at my side.

"Go get my harness from the toy box. Choose your favorite dildo. And don't forget the oil and protection."

"Yes, Mistress."

Eagle's eyes widened at the word *dildo*. Good. My lips curled at the thought of pegging that firm ass. I pulled my lower lip down into my mouth as it curled upward.

His eyes latched onto the curl of my lip. He took in a deep breath. When he exhaled, his breath reached my nostrils. The air he blew out pushed the tension out of his face, his shoulders. His big body settled before me, open and welcoming as he gazed at my grin.

The fucker. He was going to let me do it. All because he'd seen how it turned me on. Now, I exhaled. My nostrils flared as I blew a hot breath across his face.

Toy came back with the harness and dildo. I stood and strapped the device around my hips, securing the straps tight. I planned to be rough tonight and I didn't want any slippage. Then I hefted the pink, monster cock and locked it into place.

It was barely perceptible. If I hadn't been staring at him, if I'd chosen that second to blink, I would have missed it. Eagle inhaled and gulped. The chips were back in my corner. I was going to win this game.

"Oil yourself up, baby girl."

Toy did as she was told. She squirted a healthy dollop of oil in the palm of her hand. Then she rubbed her pussy and her ass in preparation.

"Toy, mount him."

Victoria did as she was told. She gave Eagle a gentle nudge. He unfolded his big body and lay down on the floor. Toy climbed on top of him. She rolled a condom over his straining dick.

Eagle smiled up at her as she worked. His gaze was kind and tender. He held her hips as she positioned her pussy over his cockhead. Then he guided her slowly as she descended down, down, down his long length.

Halfway to her end goal, Toy groaned deep in her chest. Her downward motion halted, and she took a deep breath.

"Come on, precious girl," Eagle coaxed. "You can do it."

She slid down another inch and had to stop again. This time her head lolled back as she moaned.

"Almost there," he said. "We want to make Mistress proud, don't we?"

Toy nodded her head. She took another deep breath and slid farther and farther down until Eagle was fully seated inside her.

"That's a good girl." Eagle swiped her hair away from her face and tucked it behind her ear. While Toy took a few moments to get her body adjusted to the wide, thick girth of him, Eagle glanced over her shoulder and looked at me as though he were waiting for further instructions.

"Go on," I said. "Fuck her."

"Yes, ma'am."

His dick retreated slowly. He was so thick that he stretched Toy's pussy lips and they thinned as he pulled out of her. His dick came to the end of its rope, the bulbous part of his cockhead peeked out of Toy's cunt. He held the head, the thickest part of his cock, at her entrance. Toy squirmed, but Eagle's hold was absolute.

Her slickness slid down the sides of the condom like Toy's cunt was an ice cube and his cock was the flame. She dripped down the sides of his shaft but he continued to hold her still. I saw the veins of his shaft popping out. I saw the rough skin of his ball sack shift and coil like the scales of a snake just waiting to strike. But he held still.

He held still while Toy trembled above him. I felt my own body trembling. I looked up, and that's when I saw the reason he held still. He was watching me, waiting for me.

The moment he held my gaze he shoved into my toy and she cried out. I felt my own cunt shake from the impact. Instead of letting my pussy clench in orgasmic bliss like I knew he wanted me to, I got down on my knees and threw myself into this game of chicken.

I entered Toy's oiled ass the next time Eagle was fully seated inside. My girl took us both like a champ. I'd been working both her tiny holes since I'd first met her. She was a DP princess.

From opposite ends we double penetrated her. We stroked inside of her, neither of us taking our eyes off each other. Eagle slowed down and went for deep strokes that pushed his dick so far into Toy that his balls rubbed my thigh.

Not one to be out done, I reached down and flicked a switch on the monster cock attached to my groin. The dildo woke up and began its dance. The next time Eagle's balls came near me, he caught the good vibrations.

He cursed under his breath. Score one for me. But I soon lost count of the points.

We both rammed our cocks deep into our respective channels. We fucked through Toy trying to fuck one another. Toy was a quivering, whimpering mess between us as we filled her; Eagle's cock touching her cervix and my cock vibrating deep into her ass.

At one point, Toy came so hard she passed out. Her body slumped down onto Eagle's chest. But neither he nor I stopped fucking into her.

Tears pricked the corners of my eyes from trying to hold my orgasm at bay. I'd wanted to come again since I'd turned the vibrating function of the dildo on, but I'd held on, waiting for him to blow first. I was a master of my orgasms, but I felt like I was being whipped by the desire burning in my loins.

Below me, Eagle fared no better. His teeth were grit as his thrusting became less finessed and more jerky. He was going to blow. Any minute now. And when he did I could finally give into the sweet release I so desperately wanted.

With just the thought of an orgasm, I lost

control. The contractions began in my head and made a beeline for my pussy then zinged to my clit and burst throughout my whole body. Not a half second later, I heard Eagle growl with his release. My last conscious thought was that this race would have to be declared a photo finish.

The orgasm continued to wrack my body as I rolled over and off Toy. I lay on the floor, my limbs shaking as though I'd been delivered an electric shock. I lay there for long moments, trying to come down.

Toy lay passed out between us. If I hadn't seen her chest rising and falling, I would've thought we'd killed the poor girl.

After what seemed like days of lying there, Eagle gathered Toy up into his arms. Her limbs flopped out like a rag doll's. He climbed the stairs slowly on the legs of a newborn fawn. I followed with equally wobbly legs.

We brought Toy to her bedroom. I pulled the sheets aside while Eagle tucked her under. We switched off the light and left her to her dreams.

"May I take a shower?" he asked me.

I nodded, and then guided him down the hall. I felt his hot gaze on my ass, but I was too tired to put my usual switch into my walk. I was too busy concentrating on staying up right.

I opened the door to my bedroom and led him into the en suite. He stepped past me, turning the knobs of the faucet on. He tested the waters with his fingertips. When the temperature satisfied him, he turned back to me. He held out his hand to me, like he was asking me to dance or mount his white horse and ride off into the sunset.

I'd seen a slew of men, and a couple of women, go in and out of my mother's chaotic life. I wasn't waiting for someone to swoop in and save me. I didn't believe in happily-ever-after. But an hour ago I hadn't believed in unicorns either.

What the hell? It was just a shower. I took his hand and climbed in after him.

The warm spray cooled my sensitized skin. Eagle's palms filled with suds that slicked across my body. His touch wasn't sexual. It was sensual, but it wasn't urging me toward a climax. It was lulling me to relax, and I did.

He gave me a gentle nudge into the full spray of the shower. All my worries and cares were wiped away and sent down the drain along with the suds. With my body clean and my spirit renewed, I turned and did the same to him.

I let my fingers explore his large, lean body. He was a perfect specimen, and I was one to know. I'd studied the human body academically as well as socially. I'd seen under skin and tissue. I bet that if I pulled back the layers of this man to expose muscle and bone I would find the same level of perfection.

Eagle turned the faucets off. We climbed out of the basin, and he toweled me off, carefully. Again, his machinations weren't sexual. They were careful of my sensitive skin. They were gentle and thorough about the business of removing the moisture from my body, not adding to it.

When he was done, he wrapped the damp towel around his own waist. He led me back into my bedroom, and pulled the covers of my bed down. I slipped inside, scooting over to make enough room for him. Instead of coming under the covers, he tucked them around my chest.

"Do you wanna stay over?" I asked.

"I'm tired," he said, shaking his head. "I need to get some sleep, and I don't sleep well in strange beds."

Eagle brushed a strand of hair off my face, much like he'd done for Toy. I felt myself heating, but not in the good way. The heat rose to my cheeks not in my groin.

"Thank you," he said. "Tonight was amazing, exactly what I needed. I'll have your car ready in the morning. Good night, Cleo."

He leaned down and kissed my forehead. Then he stood and padded across the floor and out the door. I heard him as he went down the stairs. I strained to hear him in the living room putting his clothes on, and then the soft snick of the door as he left. Then there was silence in the house and in my head as I lay in my bed sated and alone.

What the fuck just happened?

SEVENTEEN

I woke up the next morning in a mess of sheets. My body was hot. My head was fuzzy. My pussy throbbed with delight, but my chest itched from a phantom pain.

I dressed for work and then trudged down the stairs. Toy was up and about. She was both a morning person, and a night person. Regular sleep wasn't really her thing. She was catlike in that respect, napping at odd times of the day and waking with bursts of energy.

She'd made breakfast and cleaned. She was always on her best behavior when she wanted a reward. The reward she wanted was clearly Eagle. I didn't want to admit that I wanted him too.

Never had I ever fucked someone without

touching them. Never had I ever come so hard from someone watching me while I was fucking. Never had I ever been so thirsty while watching someone else fucking.

Bottom line; I needed to fuck this dude, and quick, to get him out of my system. I always got bored after I had them. He would be no different.

I looked at my watch. I'd have to get to work soon. As I walked to the front door, I realized I wasn't sure how I was going to get to work. Eagle and I hadn't made plans for when he'd be here, or if he'd be here to pick me up. I passed through the hall, which had a view out the living room window. What I saw in the driveway made my mouth go dry.

It was my car. I pulled the door open to get a better view. Sure enough, the dent in the front end was gone. The car glistened as though it'd been buffed and painted. My stomach clenched.

Was this some sort of payment? Had he just used me? Had he just had his fun with me and my toy and then was off.

But no. I'd had as much of an effect on him as he'd had on me. I'd brought that man to his knees last night. I'd made him sweat and pant. His eyes had filled with desire. His mouth had watered and his cock had strained for me. Hadn't it?

I didn't know what to do with all this uncertainty. So, I climbed into the driver's seat and pulled off. I was a menace on the road, cutting people off, and ignoring the speed limit. I reached the hospital and was immediately confronted with problems as the Interim Nursing Manager for the ER. As the issues came at me, my confusion about Eagle went to the back of my mind.

Until he came into the sliding glass doors with a beautiful, curvy woman on his arm. His hazel eyes looked down at her in adoration and amusement. The brunette, who was in a sundress and heels straight out of the fifties, looked up at him smiling and giggling. The young woman's hand wrapped around his elbow like he escorted her, like she was something precious.

The burning sensation from this morning returned to my chest. Along with it came a pain at the side of my face. It didn't go away after I unclenched my jaw. Eagle looked up and caught my eye. That devilish grin spread across his face and he winked. I looked away. When I looked back, they were gone.

"Excuse me?"

My gaze snapped back to the front. Then my head tilted back, way back. A tall drink of water stood before me. He was dressed for business at the bottom, but his torso was covered with a leather, motorcycle jacket at the top. The black jacket highlighted his creamy cocoa skin.

"I'm looking for Christopher Trent's room?"

The man had the type of voice that rumbled through you; a cross between Darth Vader and Idris Elba.

"I'll take you," I said feeling the nurses swarm at my back to get close to this guy.

We fell into step. I felt his cool gaze checking me out, but not with interest. It was more the habit of a man. I did the same to him out of habit. This guy was an impenetrable mountain. He didn't look like the kind to break.

"You one of Crow's brothers?" I asked.

"Not by blood. I'm Eagle's brother. My name's Yohaness."

"Excuse me? Did you say your name was Your Highness?"

"Pretty much." He looked down at me with a grin.

And then I saw it. The devil was in this man just as much as it was in his brother. There was a maturity about him though, so I had to assume Eagle was his younger brother.

"My mother believes in the power of names," he said.

"Mine, too. I'm Cleopatra. I have two brothers; Solomon and Khan."

"She named you all after various kings and queens."

"Yeah, depending on our dad's heritage. Your mom named your brother Eagle?"

"No, she didn't." He smiled, but didn't give up Eagle's given name.

"It's nice to meet you, Yohaness."

"No one calls me that. Everyone calls me Prince."

We'd arrived at Crow's room. Deep bellied laughter drifted out into the hallway accompanied by a high trill of feminine delight.

"Keep talking to my baby sister like that and I will hurt you."

I recognized the distinct growl of Eagle's bald-headed brother, the one they called Hawk.

"Do I look like I'm stupid enough to make a move on your sister?" asked Crow.

I looked again at the prim and proper young lady in the sundress. So she was Hawk's little sister; the one who played the cello. The pressure in my chest eased now that I thought back to the look Eagle had given her. It hadn't been a look of interest. It had been tender.

"My fiancée aside," Crow was saying, "I don't have a death wish."

"Can you imagine what it was like growing up with two guard dogs?" Hawk's sister punched Eagle in his arm. Eagle feigned pain, but I knew better. It was a love tap compared to what I'd done to him last night.

"Don't you mean three?" Eagle looked up to his brother who framed the door.

I watched something cross the young woman's face. It was clear the boys didn't see it. It was something only another girl would notice. The look was gone in a fleeting moment and blandness covered her pretty features. It was the lightening fast shift of emotion that caught my attention. She didn't want Prince to know that she was affected.

"Yohaness," she said, a polite airiness infused her tone as she looked up at him. "I didn't know you were in town."

Beside me Prince said nothing. I felt the tension rolling off him in waves. His lips pressed together and his eyes narrowed. He didn't move, not a single muscle, as he stared at her.

"I'm surprised you weren't the first person he

called," said Hawk, seemingly oblivious to the tension between the two. "He's always been wrapped around your little finger since you were born."

"I don't have his new number," she said with quiet accusation. In the blink of an eye, her smile returned. "Listen, I'm going to get out of your hair." She leaned over and gave Crow a kiss on the forehead. "I'm glad you're well, Christopher. Maybe slow down next time."

"Ha ha." Crow grinned. "You coming to my homecoming party tonight?"

"No." Hawk, Eagle, and Prince all said in unison.

"Just like old times," she said turning to me. "I wasn't allowed in their fort as a kid either."

She put her body in motion. Though she was short, her long legs struck the floor with purpose. She strutted like she was on a runway that was headed straight for Prince. He weaved away from the doorway like he was bracing for impact. But she didn't stop at him. She walked right past him.

When she got past his shoulder, she turned back to him. "It was good to see you again, Prince."

"You too, Gabby."

It was only a two second stare. None of the other

men caught it. But I stood right in the pathway of the heat between these two and it felt like an hour in the sauna. Gabby flipped her lush hair over her shoulder and walked out. Prince's gaze stayed stuck on her retreat.

Well played, I thought, admiring Gabby's technique. If Prince had at some point unraveled himself from her finger, he was wrapped back around it now.

"Prince, you're coming to the party tonight, right?"

Prince didn't turn to address Crow. His gaze stayed locked down the hall on the retreating figure. "I'm too old to be going to any of your parties."

"How long are you in town for?" Hawk asked him.

"Not long," he responded absentmindedly. "I just have some questions to ask you about the race."

"You think you can prosecute those dipshits for a hate crime?" Crow asked.

It took Prince a moment to respond. When he did, he didn't even bother turning around to address the room. "Listen, can I give you a call and talk about the case later?" His feet were in motion before he stopped speaking.

"Sure thing," Crow called to his retreating back.

There was a moment of silence as Prince ran

down the hall after Gabby and disappeared out of sight. Then the room filled with the sounds of male laughter.

"Poor Prince." Crow chuckled, his shoulders shaking. "He is going down, for real, this time. Gabby is about to lock that up."

"Was there ever any doubt?" asked Hawk. "My sister always gets what she wants."

"And she's wanted Prince since before she could talk," Eagle said and then laughed.

Wow, so they weren't as clueless as I thought. They saw the tension, too. Probably had for years. I wondered what was keeping Gabby and Prince apart? But I let that thought go when Eagle swaggered up to me.

"Hey," he said leaning against the doorframe, taking up the spot his brother had vacated.

"Hi." I wanted to choke on that single syllable. It came out of me breathy and airy, like I was some infatuated miss.

"You busy tonight?"

"I get off at six."

His lower lip quirked up. "Wanna get off after that?"

There went that irritation in my heart again. My mouth and my cunt flooded with warmth as I basked under his gaze. I didn't trust my mouth. Either more air or a gurgling sound from all the moisture collecting inside me would come out of it if I opened it. Instead, I nodded my head.

"Come play at my house," he said. "Bring Toy."

I didn't want to wait. I wanted to take him into one of the private patient rooms, or the supply closet, or, hell, close the door and shove Crow aside on the bed.

"What is it about you?" I shook my head, puzzling over this man. "You are so not my type."

"Two intact balls?"

I actually fucking giggled. What was going on with me?

"Sometimes like attracts like," he said.

I dipped out of the room before I did something else embarrassing, like kiss him on the mouth.

EIGHTEEN

"You can close your eyes the whole way."

Toy looked down at the floor. Her chest rose and fell in shallow pants. Her hands were balled in fists at her sides.

"Eagle will be there," I coaxed. "He wants you to come... in more ways than one."

Her fingers unfurled, but I knew that wasn't a sign of relaxation. All ten of the digits began to shake. I didn't want an episode, not when I was all dolled up in my finest leather and ready to go out.

"Okay, baby girl." I enfolded her into my arms. Slowly, her panting and shaking ceased and she relaxed into my hold. "You stay home. I'll go visit with Eagle. If you get your work done on your new project, I'll see if he'll come over this weekend to play. Okay?"

I felt her nod her head with her face buried in my neck. I let her go and she slunk down the hall. My heart hurt as I watched her go. I hated to leave her behind, but I wasn't about to pass up a night out after I'd been working so hard.

I headed for the door. On the hall table was today's mail. Amongst the regular bills, coupons, and junk mail was an ominous envelope. I opened and found a Notice to Quit inside. I cursed under my breath and then tossed it into the table's drawer.

It wasn't something I had to worry about now that I had the promotion. I'd have the money in a couple of weeks. I made my way to my car and started it up. I pulled out of the driveway and headed for my deserved night out.

Eagle's home was beside his place of business. The Watchers Crew garage was in a mixed-use part of town. One side of the street was industrial businesses. The other side were homes.

I knew which house to head for without looking down at the directions. Muscle cars lined the block. Women clad in little to no clothing made their way into the front door. I parked my car and followed the trail.

I walked down a long hall with panties and skirts littering the way. Entering the main room, most women and men were naked or nearly nude. There was a lot of blowing going on.

Crow sat in a reclining chair with a blanket over him and Mary Katherine hovering at his side. I wanted to scold. He should be lying down in a bed. All this stimulation couldn't be good for him.

No sooner did the thought enter my mind did I release and rebuke it. I wasn't on duty here. I wasn't Nurse Cleo tonight.

I would be if I saw that his health was endangered. But I knew he'd likely be tired out within the hour and request to head up to bed. So, I waved to him and then I let it go.

On the opposite end of the room, Hawk sat in a large chair that looked like a throne. His blonde girlfriend, Ellie, was perched on his lap like a prize. Both of their eyes surveyed the room before them.

Unlike the man whose lap she sat upon, Ellie was completely naked. The pink buds of her perky tits were erect. Her flat stomach trembled in an erratic rhythm. I looked lower and saw the reason why. Hawk's hand covered her pussy. It was clear to see that two digits slid slowly in and out of her.

Ellie's eyes caught mine. It took them a moment

to focus. When she recognized me, she smiled. It was a welcoming smile. It was also filled with curiosity and a hint of an invitation.

To the side of Ellie and Hawk something caught my ear and then my eye. A girl lay on a table. Her body was nude. Her arms were flung over her head. Her legs were spread and her torso was shaking. Between her legs sat Eagle.

He held a Magic Wand in his hand. His face was screwed in concentration as he worked his magic on the girl's core.

The girl's heels bounced off the floor. Her teeth grit as she white-knuckled the edge of the table. Around her, other men and women cheered her on with words of encouragement.

"You can hold out, Tessa."

"Nah, she's going to blow."

And then she did. Tessa's hips rocked off the table, mashing into Eagle's wand. Her moan was not one of satisfaction. It sounded pained and irritated. Around her the crowd groaned, too.

"I thought she had it."

"No one's ever lasted five minutes with him."

"Nice try, Tessa," said Eagle as he reached down to help her off the table. "You good?"

Tessa took a deep breath. "Fuck you," she said.

Eagle grinned.

"Later?" she asked with a smile.

"Sure thing," he winked. Then he turned back to the crowd. "Who's playing next?" He looked around at the eager faces, and then his gaze fell on me. "Hello, Nurse Cleo. I'm glad you made it."

"What's the game?" I asked.

"Orgasm wars. There are points for who lasts the longest before coming, and then a second round where we count number of orgasms. Wanna play?"

I raised an eyebrow. If he thought I'd drop my panties and be on display in front of these strangers, he had not a clue about me.

Eagle reached to his side and produced a second Magic Wand. He turned with a grin and presented it to me. "Let's go head to head."

That itchy, tingly feeling came back to my chest as I took the wand from him. I was happy to sit down next to him because my legs were prepared to give out. My palm was sweaty as I wrapped my fingers around the vibrator. I got ahold of myself and gripped it tight as two women took their places before us.

"What are the rules?" I asked.

"Vibrator only, no hands. The vibrators must remain in contact with the skin between her legs.

You can change the settings on the vibrator, but it must remain on. Got it?"

Nodding, I turned on the vibrator and focused on the cunt in front of me. It was already dripping with anticipation. I felt like I'd been given the lame horse in the race. But somehow, I knew better. Eagle would never take an advantage for himself. He'd want to win fair and square. His girl was foaming at the lower lips, too.

"Start the clock," he said. "And go."

I aimed the vibrator straight for my contestant's clit. She must have been expecting me to play around in her inner thighs like Eagle was doing to his girl. My girl's eyes went wide as the head of the wand met her bud. Her mouth gaped open and her legs began trembling.

"I'm going to come," she warned.

"I know, sweetheart," I said.

"But...but..." She could barely get words out. I could see the vibrations traveling down her legs as they shook. Her belly trembled. Her fingers shook. Her teeth chattered and her eyes rolled back in her head. "I can't hold it."

"Then don't, honey. You should do what feels good."

Eagle looked at me with a grin. "You're going to lose."

"I never lose."

I held his gaze as the girl who was spread out before me erupted into orgasm. My brow quirked up in challenge. Eagle's eyes narrowed in suspicion.

"Round two?" I asked.

I left the vibrator on my girl as she continued to convulse on the table.

Eagle looked from her dripping pussy to my face. "Second round lasts for five minutes. Whoever gets their pussy to come the most in that time frame wins."

"And we add the amount of orgasms in the second round to the first?"

His gaze narrowed as he realized my tactic. "That first blow doesn't count."

It didn't matter. Once you got the first orgasm out of the way, the next one or two or more were much easier.

"You can change your weapon," he said. "But you only get one."

"Do fingers count as one weapon?"

"Yes, they do."

I sat down my wand. So did he.

"Start the clock," I said.

He grinned. "Let's play."

As soon as the time started I inserted my fingers into the cunt that was my game board. I searched around in the front of the girl's pussy, crooking my fingers in a come-hither motion, until I found the spot I was looking for. I began to massage.

I looked over to see that Eagle was doing the same. It was going to be a matter of technique.

His girl came first, her body jerking and undulating under his skilled touch. My girl came second. Having been primed for an orgasm already by her first blow, she was ripe to keep blossoming. Right on the heels of her second orgasm, another smaller orgasm kicked into gear.

Not to be outdone, Eagle pulled a second orgasm from his girl. Then he flipped her over so that her belly was on the table and her ass was presented to him. He stuck his fingers back inside her and pumped the living daylights out of her.

It was a smart technique. I would've done it myself if my girl hadn't already come twice from manipulation. I needed a different technique. I pulled my fingers out of her cunt and gave her swollen lips a slap.

She yelped and jerked. I did it again, and then again. When she was the darkest shade of pink, I grabbed her clit with my thumb and index finger and squeezed her bud hard enough for it to pop. And pop it did, she came all over my hand.

Before she came down, I stuck my fingers back into her cunt and pulled another orgasm out of her channel. Moaning and slapping, pinching and squeezing continued all around me. I couldn't tell who was coming and from where. A buzzer went off somewhere close and someone called, "Time."

I looked up. There was a posterboard where someone had kept a tally. I looked at Eagle's name. He had four tick marks. Under my name there was a block. It took me a moment to realize it was four marks with a slash that equaled five.

I'd won.

Eagle didn't look the least bit put out that I'd won at his game. He had that look in his eye; that look he'd gotten in the stairwell when he'd been deep throating Nurse Charity; that look he'd gotten when he'd pumped into Toy while staring at me. It was that look that said, *is this what you want?*

Just like last night, he was doing this to turn me on, to get a rise out of me. And it was working. I'd been trying to win with the pieces laid out in front of me, but he was playing an entirely different game. I was not about to play into his hands.

"Two out of three?" I asked.

His smile told me that I did not disappoint him. I tried not to let that make my nipples hard, but my clit still tingled at the flash of his teeth.

He turned from me and looked at the gathered crowd. "Who's next?"

NINETEEN

A few hours later, Eagle and I stood under the spray of a warm shower. He washed my body the same way he'd done the other night. He wasn't trying to get a rise out of me, but my temperature rose anyway.

He squirted liquid soap into a luffa. Then he squeezed the suds onto the side of my neck. The foamy water dripped down onto my shoulder. Eagle caught the frothy mix of soap and water with his palm. He curled his fingers into my shoulder and massaged my skin, my muscles.

His hands brought the luffa and soap to my chest. He cupped my breasts. He didn't toy with my nipples. Instead, he wiped the cum and squirt juices from my skin.

The orgasm games had gone on until we'd felled everyone in the line. I'd lost track of the points. My attention had only been on the task at hand and making a note of how Eagle's nostrils flared as he watched me work.

Now his hands glided down to my belly and circled around my back. I leaned into him as he lathered my torso and then my ass. His hands worked magic but I was more enthralled with the feel of his shoulderblade and the comfort I found there as the water trickled over his shoulder and onto my cheek.

He let me rest there on his chest as he turned the luffa on himself and wiped the carnal activities from his own body. Then we stood under the spray and let the water wash it all away.

As the droplets continued to fall, and Eagle's heartbeat sounded in my ear, my limbs grew loose, my muscles heavy. My breathing slowed and all the tension from the last week melted away. I knew I should probably leave, but I would've been happy to stay in the basin for the rest of the night.

"Tired?" he asked as he pulled a towel around me.

I nodded, lifting my head off his chest with great effort.

"Wanna sleep here?"

I opened my mouth, and then shut it. Was this another power play? When I'd asked him to sleep with me, he'd refused. But the last thing I wanted was to drive home. Hell, I didn't even want to go back downstairs.

"You can sleep in my bed." He held my palm as he handed me out of the tub. It reminded me of how gentlemen in Victorian England would escort ladies about.

"I thought you didn't like strangers in your bed."

"No, I don't like to sleep in strange beds."

He guided me to his bed. It was a large, queen-sized bed. The wood of the four posters was mahogany and the comforter was royal purple. Eagle pulled back the covers, and just like he'd handed me out of the shower, he handed me into the bed.

I sank into the depths of the mattress. He pulled the sheets over my body and then his large, warm body spooned me from behind. My nipples tightened and my pussy tingled. "Did you want to have sex?"

I couldn't see his face. He'd buried his head between my shoulderblades and pulled my back snug into his chest.

"I'm tapped out," he said. I could feel his lips form a smile as they brushed the space where my neck met the center of my shoulder blades. "I'd rather my first time with you be one of my best performances."

"I'm tapped out, too."

"We can just sleep."

"Okay."

I was out before I finished the second syllable of that word. It was the most fitting sleep I'd had in a long time. Which was strange because I didn't particularly like sleeping with others.

I was a light sleeper and every move a bed partner made would rouse me. Not so with Eagle. My body sank into his hold and I did not stir until the sunlight kissed my eyelids.

When I woke up in the morning, I was in the bed alone. I turned over and looked around the room, but Eagle was gone. I dressed in last night's clothes and headed downstairs.

The house looked like a normal home with all the naked bodies gone. There was hardly a trace of the debauchery that had gone down the night before. The floors were cleared of underwear. The food and drinks were gone from the side tables. But I smelled something heavenly down the hall and I headed for the kitchen.

Eagle stood at the stove with a spatula in one

hand and the handle of a pan in the other. There was a stack of waffles and something that looked like crepes on the counter. The Asian guy, Owl, I'd learned his name was, squeezed oranges into a strainer.

Sitting around the island were the blonde Ellie, prim Mary Katherine, and dark-skinned Kira. Eagle piled more breakfast foods onto the women's plates, while Owl filled their glass tumblers with fresh orange juice.

"Good morning, Cleo," Eagle said when he saw me standing in the entryway.

I was greeted with enthusiasm from everyone present and then ushered onto a barstool by Ellie.

"Are you hungry?" Ellie asked. "Eagle makes the best waffles and crepes."

"Eagle cooks?"

Eagle grinned as he piled both items onto a plate along with sausage. He turned and presented the dish to me and then leaned over the counter to watch me eat. I met his gaze as I sliced into one of the crepes. Then I closed my eyes and moaned as the fluffy, buttery treat melted on my tongue.

Eagle chuckled and turned back to the stove to make more.

I turned and each of the women gave me a

knowing look as they pulled forks from their own mouths. I took another bite, wondering if I'd woken up in heaven.

"Hey." Hawk's massive frame filled the door. "Mrs. Robinson's here for a tune up." He made a beeline for Ellie, nuzzling her neck and stealing a sausage from her plate.

"Kira and I are headed out," said Owl.

"Crow wore himself out last night at the party," said MK. "He's not getting out of bed anytime soon."

Eagle turned off the burners and then turned to me. "Cleo, you think you can give us a hand with this job?"

I looked between Eagle and Hawk. "I'm useless when it comes to cars. I can't even change my own tire."

Hawk grinned and tilted his head, indicating that I should follow them out the door. Eagle, Hawk, Ellie and I made our way across the yard and to the Watchers Crew garage. Inside the garage a mature woman dressed in a designer blouse and skirt leaned against a Lexus.

"What seems to be the problem today, Mrs. R?" asked Eagle.

"I can't seem to get her to start."

I rounded the hood of the car. I knew enough to

know that if the hood was hot then the engine was running, the woman had just driven here. It quickly became clear to me that this appointment had nothing to do with cars.

"Let's get a look under the hood and see what we're working with." This came from Hawk. His massive hands tugged up Mrs. Robinson's shirt while Eagle tugged her skirt down. The woman was bare beneath her clothes. They hefted her up onto the hood of her car.

"Can I take a look?" I asked.

Hawk looked over his shoulder. Then he looked to Mrs. Robinson. There was interest in her eyes. Hawk stepped aside and let me between Mrs. Robinson's legs.

I parted her thighs and peered inside. "You like feeling full, don't you Mrs. Robinson?"

I kept my nails trim not only because of my work in the ER and having to wear my fair share of latex. I kept my nails trim because I liked to shove my fingers into all manner of things -mouths, asses, and pussies to name my favorites.

I inserted three fingers into Mrs. Robinson's cunt to start with. She gasped, but gave no resistance. I worked my way up to my knuckles, pumping her g-spot to get her to relax even further.

I rocked my hand back and forth, reaching my fingertips to the internal skin behind her clit. On the exit, I bared down with my knuckles, stretching her opening even wider. When she gave, I squeezed in my pinkie finger.

With four fingers inside Mrs. Robinson, I began rotating my wrist. I went slowly; fairly certain that this was her first time having someone's hand inside of her. Dicks, for all their hardness, were still pretty malleable. But my fingers had four hard bones pressing up and down inside her.

Mrs. Robinson arched up into my hand and I knew I could go deeper. I slid my thumb in to meet my other four fingers. I thrusted and retreated, going deeper each time, until I had my whole hand inside of her cunt.

"Holy fuck."

The whisper came from behind me. I couldn't tell if it was Hawk or Eagle. A glance over my shoulder showed me that Ellie clung to Hawk. Her thighs were pressed together, her mouth hung open, and her eyes were fastened to the hand that was pumping inside Mrs. Robinson.

Hawk clung to Ellie, watching my technique as though he were taking notes for later.

Eagle's gaze was fixed on me. Not on my hand.

Not on Mrs. Robinson's shaking thighs. He was watching the expression on my face.

I gave him a grin and a wink that said *watch this*. I turned back to the cunt before me. I tilted Mrs. Robinson's pelvis up with my free hand and sped up my motions. Her back arched up and she threw her head back. Her eyes rolled around and her entire body began to tremble.

Her muscles tried to push me out as she began to come, but I held my ground. Her channel grabbed at me, convulsing all around my fingers, my palm, and my wrist. It was the gush of fluids that finally pushed me out.

A geyser of fluids sprang from somewhere deep inside of Mrs. Robinson. It poured out of her in great gushes that rendered her mute. She couldn't moan, or groan, or shout. Her hands balled into fists. Her shoulders collapsed. Her upper body gave out, and still her pussy gushed.

She hadn't pushed me all the way out. Four of my fingers were still inside of her, thrusting away and keeping the flow going. The slurping sounds of a wet pussy working filled the garage. The only other sounds were Ellie's low mewls and Hawk's heavy breathing. Eagle and I remained mute' as Mrs. Robinson came down.

When Mrs. Robinson collapsed down onto the hood of her car, I pulled my hand from her pussy. "Did that fix the problem?" I asked.

"Yes, dear," she whispered. "I think that was just the service I needed."

As Mrs. Robinson slowly and carefully stood and put herself back together, I turned to face Eagle. He wore my favorite look; one of complete reverence.

TWENTY

Unfortunately, work got in the way of my plans to fuck Eagle. I left the Watchers Crew garage with a pep in my step, and a snap in my fisting fingers. I called to check on Toy. She was doing well so I didn't stop home. I headed straight to the hospital in my party clothes.

I had spare scrubs in the locker room. I was barely out of the locker room door when the nurses bombarded me with problems. I took a deep breath and slid into a seat at the nurse's station. Gone were the days where I could sneak off with one of the attendings for a quickie in the break room.

I headed to Wanda's office to gather up some forms I needed. Even though she was out, she usually left her door open and her files locked. She'd left me a key.

When I rounded the corner, I saw her door was not only open, but it was filled with a few bodies. Inside I saw the Chief and a couple of doctors crowded around Wanda's desk. Maybe Wanda had recovered?

I stepped inside and saw that Wanda was indeed sitting behind her desk. Her eyes were a bit puffy, her nose a little red. She wasn't smiling. In fact, she looked a bit hostile. Her glare was directed at Chief Rowe.

Wanda's gaze shifted when she spotted me, and I saw her inhale. She pressed her hands together and gave a shake of her head. Then like a domino, the others turned and saw me. Whatever conversation had been going on hushed as I crossed the threshold.

"Hello," I said into the silence.

Wanda's jaw tightened and she looked away from me.

"I'm due in surgery soon," said Dr. West. He slunk out of the door without making any eye contact with me.

Dr. Page stood in a corner. He leaned his shoulder against a bookshelf as though he was getting settled in for a good show.

Chief Rowe cleared his throat and stepped to me. "I'm glad you're here, Cleo."

I arched an eyebrow at him.

He cleared his throat and began again, but still incorrectly. "You've met Sister Ruth."

I peered beside him. Sitting quietly in an office chair was the nun, clothed head to toe in her habit. She stood and nodded towards me.

"Sister Ruth has just accepted the role of Head of Nursing in the ER."

I ran his words in my head over and over again. Sister Ruth had accepted what?

I kept my glare on him as I tried in vain to make sense of his words. Chief Rowe shifted and loosened his tie. Wanda sat back with her arms crossed over her chest. Dr. Page smirked in the corner.

"I'm excited to work with you, Nurse Cleo." Sister Ruth rose and approached me. "I'm sure I'll need your help as this merger goes forth."

I stared at her face. There was no mirth there like in Page's. Page was happy to see me get what I assumed he thought was my just desserts since I never gave him any of my treats.

There was no trepidation in Sister Ruth's peaceful face like there was in Chief Rowe's. He was waiting for me to explode. Tension rippled through his forearms as though he was preparing to duck and take cover at a moment's notice.

There was no resignation in the holy woman's face like there was in Wanda's. Wanda's features screamed *I told you so*. She'd warned me to play nice with the men I worked with.

I wished I had their dicks out and in cock cages so that I could swallow the keys and watch them suffer from frustration. I wished I had them all bent over my knee so that I could punish them with a spanking. Instead, I was the one left frustrated. I was the one being punished. I was the one who was powerless in this position.

I looked around the room. It was a bit of a shock to realize that, though I'd made Rowe my bitch years ago, though I'd helped out Page, though I'd taken on more than my fair share for Wanda, I didn't have a single ally. No one had my back.

I stepped back, away from the nun who had stepped into my place. Sister Ruth didn't look like she'd ever hurt a fly. But she'd been placed on the gameboard and she'd beaten me. There was only one card that I had left to play.

"You won't get any help from me, sister. I quit." I turned and walked out the door.

I was actually surprised to hear footsteps behind me. "Cleo."

I slowed for Wanda. It was clear the poor woman was still a bit under the weather. "This is bullshit, Wanda. That's my job and they're going to give it to that-"

Wanda held up her hand. "I'm Christian. Don't you dare blaspheme. And don't quit either. That gets you nowhere and it leaves us in a bind."

I huffed, crossing my arms and pacing the width of the hall like a caged tiger.

"I don't like it," said Wanda. "But we have no choice. Sacred Heart is merging with Sisters of Mercy. The hospital is doing what it has to do to survive."

"They're rolling over and doing what they're told, and that's not my style."

"No, it's not. You think everyone will just bend to your will, but you won't return the favor. I've stuck my neck out for you time after time."

"Well, you won't have to do it anymore."

I turned and marched down the hall. I heard her sigh, but she didn't follow.

TWENTY-ONE

My hands shook all the way home. I'd just quit my job. That was my way. See a small flame and throw gasoline on it so I could watch it burn. I was the very definition of a sadist. My favorite victim to inflict pain, suffering, and humiliation upon was myself.

How the hell was I going to pay our bills now? What would happen to our living situation? Why couldn't I have just accepted their decision and at least continued on with my old job? But, no. I had to burn the bridge as I switched my ass across it.

I pulled onto my street. There was a car at the top of my driveway. I recognized it immediately as Eagle's. I sighed, but this exhale was one of relief. Getting Eagle on his knees, bending him to my will, was exactly the remedy I needed to cure this fucked up day. I parked in the drive and headed inside.

When I walked in, I stopped in my tracks. Eagle had Toy in his lap. He was stroking her hair and whispering to her. Toy was nodding; her eyes were wide like he was hanging the moon for her.

"What the fuck are you doing?" I demanded.

Toy's spine straightened and her head snapped up. Guilt shone dark on her face. She moved, likely to drop to the floor in supplication. But Eagle held her still in his lap. When my gaze found his, he was scowling at me.

"Hey, hey," soothed Eagle as he brought Toy back into his arms. "It's okay. Everything's going to be okay. Just like I promised."

I saw red. Who the hell did he think he was? I wasn't one to be stingy with my toys or my Toy. But I would go off if you came into my house and took my stuff without my permission.

I clenched my fists and my jaw. I took a deep breath, but it wasn't meant to calm me. No, it was meant to unleash a tirade.

I was called up short by Toy's wide-eyed look of terror. The calm that Eagle had petted into her dropped away from her face and the signs of a panic attack swarmed in. She began rocking her upper body. Tears streamed down her cheeks. She started counting primes.

Eagle didn't even blanche. He simply put his lips to her temple and made shushing noises. The sight of Toy in a panic with Eagle soothing her made all the anger drain from me.

I saw him with her in his arms and I realized that I wanted to be there instead of standing here on my own. I wanted him to tell me that everything was going to be okay. But I held my place, alone in the middle of the room.

"Your mistress and I are going to handle this," he said.

Toy had only made it to thirty-one. She'd stopped rocking. She wasn't shaking. Her eyes were open, not squeezed shut.

"Now you go and make your Mistress a cup of tea," Eagle said. "She looks like she's had a day."

Toy turned her gaze to me. Her mouth went pensive. Her eyes dipped. She didn't move.

I sighed. All of the fight gone from my bones. "Go on, baby girl."

Toy rose, head down, and went into the kitchen. Both Eagle and I watched her go. Then he turned to me with that scowl. He reached onto the table and held a paper up. It took me a moment to recognize it, but when I did I rolled my eyes skyward.

"Why didn't you tell me there was a problem?" he demanded, slamming the eviction notice down on the table.

"It's not your problem."

"If someone's got beef with you, then I'm taking a fucking bite out of it."

"You're not my family. You're a guy I fuck." I wrapped my arms around myself. Though I held still, it felt like everything around me was rocking.

And then I felt arms around me and my world went off kilter. I tried to shove him away, but my fingers got tangled in his shirt. I tried to tell him to go to hell, but my lips got lost in the valley between his pecs.

"I have everything under control," I insisted.

"Hmm," he soothed, pressing his lips against my temple and stroking my hair the same way he'd done with Toy.

"I don't need your help." But my voice was barely above a whisper since my lips were pressed against the Adam's apple in his neck. I wanted to take a bite. I was sure he'd let me.

"Well, you're gonna get my help," he growled. "Because you have lost your fucking mind if you think I'm going to stand by and watch the two of you be put out on the street. Not if there's something I can do about it."

"What if I tell you to get out?" I said.

"Okay. I'll leave."

He let me go and I nearly collapsed to the floor. I was loath to admit that for the last few minutes, it had only been his arms and his strength that had been holding me up. The second he took them away, I deflated.

"But I'm taking this." He grabbed the citation. "My mom's a judge. I'll see what she can do about it."

"Why? Why would you do that? What's it going to cost me? You want me to be your fuck slave, because I won't. I'm nobody's bitch, Eagle."

He frowned at me. His brows rose in what I had to assume was incredulity.

"I'm going to do it because you're my friend," he said. "And that's what friends do for each other. They help each other out. And they don't expect anything in return except the friendship. I might be an ass, but I'm not a villain. I'm not trying to be your hero either. Or take away your autonomy. I like your autonomy. I'd like to keep my access to it. If that means getting my mommy to pull some strings so I can keep playing with you, then so be it."

He folded up the notice and put it in his pocket. Then he slipped his leather jacket on. I may have made a sound of protest as he covered up the arms and chest that had been the only thing to bring me relief in days. When he made his way past me, I reached out and grabbed for him.

"Wait."

He paused, and turned to look at me. His lips were set in a firm line that warned me not to challenge him. But his eyes were soft as they regarded me, filled with something I hadn't seen aimed at me in a long time; compassion, kindness, and care.

Did he actually care about me? Or was I so tired and weary that I was projecting it onto him?

I didn't know. I didn't really care. I just wanted to be near it for a while longer.

"I'm coming with you," I said.

TWENTY-TWO

Eagle's mom was not what I expected. She had tightly curled hair that framed her oval-shaped head like she was a queen. Her wide eyes narrowed on me, taking me in and holding me in place, like she was a warrior assessing a new foe.

For the first time in a long time, I was the first to look away. Judge Oluyemi Obademi was an intimidating woman. She turned her gaze back on the papers that her son had handed her after introductions.

"I'm sorry," said Judge Obademi, slapping the notice down on the large oak desk of her home office. "I can't help you."

My chest deflated and my shoulders caved in. I hated to admit that I had gotten my hopes up.

"You don't see any loophole or technicality that she can use?" asked Eagle.

His mother picked up the paper again, but even as she reached for it, she shook her head. "It looks like that property is getting purchased for development. It's worth more demolished. I take it you're not Ms. Long."

"No," I said. "Victoria is my live-in submissive."

Eagle cleared his throat.

I turned to look at him. He quirked an eyebrow at me. "I'm sorry," I said. "I don't hide my lifestyle."

I expected him to go into a huff that I'd put my kink on display in front of his mother. Instead, he lowered his brow, and the corner of his mouth rose. Warmth rushed through me. Any other guy would be ushering me out of the room, making excuses, or at least sweating bullets. Not Eagle

"Ethelbert," said his mom.

Now my eyebrows rose. "Ethelbert?"

He sighed heavily as he turned his attention back to his mother. Mrs. Obademi looked between the two of us. Her gaze lingered on her son in a question. Eagle held her gaze with a smile I'm sure got him out of chores many a time. Then the judge settled her gaze on me.

"I'm sorry, my dear, but your only option is to sell."

I shook my head. "Toy, Ms. Long, is agoraphobic. That house is her safe place."

"I see that it's her sister that's filed this paperwork," said the judge.

"She's a selfish, unfeeling bitch." And then, when silence followed my comment, I glanced over at Eagle, who had a pinched look on his face, and then to his mother, whose arched brows were nearly touching her crown of hair. "Sorry."

"In my line of work, I see a lot of blood relatives tear each other apart for the wrong reasons," said Mrs. Obademi. "It's not often that I see individuals fight for one another for the right reasons. It looks like that's what you have here with your...Toy. The best I can do for you is to tie up the paperwork for another week or two, give you a chance to find some place new."

"Thank you." I stood to rise, but felt something tethered to me, which slowed my progress. It was Eagle's hand. His fingers slid inside my fists. Then his fingers slid between each of mine. He was holding my hand.

"Thank you, Mama," he said as he leaned over the desk and kissed his mother on the cheek.

"I would like you home for dinner one night this week while your brother's in town," said his mother.

"Yes, ma'am."

Mrs. Obademi's gaze turned to me. "You can bring your...friend."

Eagle tugged me out of the door and then out of the house before I could respond. His hand was the only thing holding me up. When he let my fingers go, I nearly protested. But his arm came around my shoulder and his hand gripped my forearm. I felt completed, supported, and entirely frightened.

I had screwed everything up, but somehow there were arms around me. I couldn't remember the last time I'd been held. I was so weary that I let Eagle wrap me up in his arms.

He wasn't trying to sweep me off my feet. He was holding me up, helping me to stand strong on my own two feet. My forehead came to rest on his chin. He kissed my temple and told me it was going to be okay. My body betrayed me and I gave him all of my weight.

"I quit my job today," I said.

"Yeah?"

"They gave someone else my promotion."

"Then they were stupid." His stubble brushed my ear as he spoke.

"I was stupid. I shouldn't have quit. Now I need to look for a new place and I don't even have the money to do it."

"You know you two can come and stay with us."

I sighed, shaking my head. "Toy could never handle being around that many people on a daily basis."

Eagle caressed my back and shoulders, just like he'd done in the shower. It wasn't sexual. It was just to make me feel good. It was such a foreign feeling. I realized then that I had been intimate with this guy on more than one occasion, but I'd never actually fucked him.

"I assume you won't take any money from me either?" he said.

"You assume right."

"Not even if it was a loan and I charged you a stupid amount of interest?"

"You're not a stupid guy."

"What if I knew of a job opening that could use your special set of skills. It pays a stupid amount of money. But it's not always legal."

I leaned back and looked into his handsome face. We stood just outside his family's front door. The porch light backlit him and he looked like he was glowing in his leather jacket. A dark night in shining Armani.

"I keep expecting you to disappoint me or turn on me," I said. "Can you hurry up and do it so that I can stop being so anxious."

"If I fucked you over, would you let me anywhere near your pussy?"

"No."

"There's your guarantee."

TWENTY-THREE

We were out in the middle of nowhere, as this was not a sanctioned race. My job was as a part of the medical staff in the very likely event of an accident. If an ambulance was called, the patient would be taken to a hospital and then, likely, to jail afterwards. I'd already been handed a fat wad of cash for my services. It wasn't enough to keep the house, but it was enough for a security deposit on an apartment.

I stood in the medical tent and spied Eagle in the distance. He leaned under his car's hood with Hawk at his side. He wore a dark jumpsuit that clung to his athletic form. I pulled my bottom lip in with my teeth thinking about how much I wanted to be that jumpsuit.

With my pre-race duties done, I wandered away

from the tent. Scantily clad women sashayed through the stands, leaning over the railings and brandishing their tits and asses. They weren't just eyeing the male hot rods on the track; they were scoping each other out as well. There was curiosity in their eyes as they fell on me.

A lot of the men gathered leered at me even though I was in my scrubs. I arched a brow at each of them. I curled my lips at the ones who didn't immediately drop their gazes. I made a mental catalogue of the ones whose pupils dilated with interest.

Walking around, I completely understood the draw of the racing world. This was a virtual playground. I wasn't interested in the speed of the cars. I was interested in new playmates.

Without even planning it, I ended up at the Watchers Crew car. Two women stood nearby arguing.

"You sucked his dick at the last race and look where that got him," said a redhead with thick, ruby lips.

The second woman, a brunette, put her hands on her barely covered hips and glared at the redhead. The red head cocked her head and her gaze shifted to me. The brunette turned and they both glared.

"There's already a line," said the redhead.

"For?" I asked.

"To suck Eagle off before the race," said the brunette. "You know, for luck."

Before I could respond, I felt a hand come to rest at my low back. Any other man and he'd have lost not only that appendage but one further south and more dear. But my body instinctively yielded to this man.

"Hey," Eagle said into my ear.

His hot breath sent a shiver down my spine. I inhaled the smell of him, already so familiar in just a couple of days. His strong chest at my back made me want to turn and curl up in the center of him.

"You good?" he asked.

His lip grazed the tip of my ear. I couldn't help myself, I leaned back. My head rested at the crook between his neck and shoulder. "Yeah. We were just debating who would get to give you your pre-race blow job."

I felt his head rise to look in front of us. "Hey Rain, Josie."

Both Rain's and Josie's gazes were fixed on the hand Eagle had wrapped around my middle.

"What did you decide?" His lips were back at my ear.

"I decided..." I turned in his hold, placing my hands on his chest and gazing into his hazel eyes. "...that two rounds of head are always better than one."

He chuckled. His eyes sparkled as he looked down at me. That dark gaze dipped to my lips as though he wanted to give my mouth some head. Instead, he tugged his bottom lip into his mouth and backed away from me slowly.

"You coming to watch?" His thumb rubbed circles on my hip before he let me go. His other four fingers dug into the start of the V that separated my thigh from my pussy.

"Can't," I said with a regretful twist of my lips. "Gotta get back to the medical tent."

Eagle's brows drew with that same turn of regret as mine. "I'll catch you after the race? I got something to show you."

"Definitely. I want a rematch at the party tonight."

His grin spread wide, replacing the regret with anticipation. "You're on."

He dipped his head. Instead of capturing my lips, he placed a lingering kiss at my cheek. When he pulled away I knew he'd missed his mark. But his intended target was territory he didn't yet have permission to enter.

Eagle turned and headed into the pit with the two girls trailing eagerly at his heels. I turned and headed back toward the medical tent. As I wove my way through the racers, someone stepped in my way.

"Hey, look who it is."

I looked up to see the passenger-side-scrub from the Nazi street race a few nights ago.

"It's the Watchers Crew mutt."

I felt like I was in a Guy Ritchie film where the hero envisions how he will kick the bad guy's ass in detailed, slow motion steps before he lifts a finger. Then time reverses and speeds up and the bad guy is on the ground in fast-forward. But this bad guy didn't go to the ground like I dreamed. I kept my fists at my sides. I'd already blown one job. I wasn't about to lose this one, too.

"Hey, soul sistah? Chica?" he said. "What the fuck are you any way?"

I took a couple of steps towards him. He was surrounded by other men who looked like carbon copies of him; shaved heads, hatred in their eyes, and menace in their faces. Their chests were puffed up like little boys playing at being men.

"What I am," I said, "is more man than you'll ever be. Come on big boy, whip it out and let's measure our dicks. See whose is bigger."

He blinked. Off to the side, someone choked on a laugh. Then another person. Passenger-Guy grit his teeth then he marched up to me. Anger and intent radiated off his jumpsuit-clad body.

As he moved towards me, he blocked out the sun. Big guys always underestimated me. I was small but I was scrappy. The perfect height to go for his groin in a way he would not find pleasurable.

Just as he was about to reach me, a massive hand came between us.

"I know you were not about to touch my brother's property." Hawk sidled up in front of me. His big body blocked out the few rays of the sun that remained.

"I am not anybody's property," I protested, though I doubted my voice carried beyond Hawk's broad shoulders.

"We've got this, Nurse Cleo," said Owl coming up beside me.

"You thought I needed help with this pansy?" I balked. "He probably can't handle his gear shift, which is why he tried to latch on to a real one." I grabbed my crotch.

There was a stunned moment of silence. Then laughter broke out all around.

"I really like her," Hawk said to Owl.

They turned, keeping me between them and escorted me back to the medical station. I glanced over my shoulder to see Passenger-Guy fuming. I smirked and turned back to my escorts.

"I had that under control," I said.

"Did you hear that shit? *Whip it out*," Hawk laughed. "That was bad ass."

"You like pasta, Nurse Cleo?" asked Owl.

"Um, yeah," I said.

"Cool, I'll make some fresh for you tonight."

"You're going to cook for me?"

"Ellie says that cooking is our love language," said Hawk.

"You don't have to do that," I started but Owl waved my protest away.

"No use fighting it," said Owl. "You're family now."

"Feels like the mafia," I said.

"No," said Owl. "You can get out of the mafia. You'll never get away from the Watchers Crew."

TWENTY-FOUR

Despite all the screaming, and shouting, and growl of motors, racing was not that exciting. The sleek cars zipped round and round the track, making left hand turn after left hand turn. I had to look away or I'd fall asleep from all the monotony. So, my back was turned when it happened.

The crash was a terrifying bang of metal and rubber and concrete and screams. I rushed down to the pavement to see two cars entwined with one another. One car bore a tire with wings. The other bore the emblem of a swastika.

My heart calmed as I heard Eagle shouting, climbing from his mangled car. His eyes connected with mine. His eyes were clear and focused. His feet were steady as he came to stand on the asphalt.

I heard one of the doctors call my name from the other car. When I turned I saw that the Passenger-Douche had a gaping wound on his head. His eyes lolled back in his head. He fought the hands that tried to free him from the wreck and his body wove and teetered as he tried and failed to gain any semblance of balance.

I wanted to run to Eagle and feel for certain that he was okay. But I didn't. I cursed under my breath, and then forced my feet to move away from Eagle.

I came up to the racist piece of shit that was seriously wounded. My quick assessment of his injuries told me that his shoulder was dislocated. It was likely that he had multiple fractures. He needed to get to a hospital as soon as possible.

It would take too long for an ambulance to make it to the race site and then double back to the hospital. The doctor, his assistant, and I piled into someone's car and sped to Sacred Heart.

The injured man was in and out of consciousness all along the way. During his brief moments of lucidness, the silence was punctuated by "Fucking Mutt" and "Get Your Jew Hands Off Me." Along with the hateful epitaphs directed at the helping hands were a lot of deep breaths and calls for Jesus by the medical professionals.

The ride felt like it took forever. But finally, the red brick face of Sacred Heart Hospital came into view. We rushed into the ER and familiar faces greeted me.

As I called out the patient's stats, he continued his despicable diatribe. Nurses that I'd worked with for years rolled their eyes and grit their teeth, but they each got down to work. It was Sister Ruth who stood stunned, gaping at the man who needed her saving grace.

And this is who they had replaced me with?

"Snap out of it," I said to her. "We can't turn him away. Even if he's a racist, misogynist, ugly asshole with a dick the size of a paperclip."

"You fucking..." but the Nazi's gaze slipped from me. "Ruth, is that you?"

Everyone's gaze turned to Sister Ruth. She gulped. Took a deep breath and then gulped again.

"All right, everyone." Her quiet voice rang loud through the hustle and bustle of the Emergency Room. "Let's get this man admitted."

They wheeled the driver away. His slurs echoed down the hall as the staff rallied to heal his wounds.

"How do you know that guy?" I asked.

"Church." Sister Ruth shut her eyes as though she didn't want to see the words that escaped from some dark place inside of her. "My father's a pastor. He preaches some pretty hateful things that never set right with me nor the God that I serve. So, I left."

She opened her eyes and her gaze connected with mine. There was a story there; one of strength and resilience. For a moment, I wanted to sit down and hear it. But I remembered she was my enemy, the reason I didn't work here any more. I turned, preparing to take a step out the door. That's when I saw him.

Eagle walked into the sliding glass doors. He still wore his tracksuit. He was flanked by Hawk and Owl. All of their faces looked grim as they searched the room.

"Nurse Cleo," said Sister Ruth who still stood beside me. "I'd like to ask you to reconsider your position here. It was evident to me the first time that I met you that you are a credit to this place. And in the last two days your absence has been felt."

Eagle's gaze finally found me. His lips pursed. I saw his nostrils flare like a bull's blowing out steam before he charged.

The saying goes that when one door closes another opens. I hadn't meant to close the door to my job at the hospital. But I was thankful that that door shutting had led me into Eagle's arms. And now that the door to Eagle would be closing after I hopped in a car to save his nemesis instead of coming to his side, I was being sent back through the hospital's sliding glass doors.

Ironic.

"I'll only work three days a week," I said to Sister Ruth, my gaze still on Eagle as he made his way to me.

"Isn't that a normal shift?" asked Sister Ruth.

"And no weekends."

"I accept," she said.

"But I can't return until next week. I have to move."

I had no idea where I'd be moving with Toy. The only place I wanted to move was back inside Eagle's arms, with his hand on my waist and his lips at the curve of my ear.

But that door was closed. I didn't hear Sister Ruth leave. I tuned everything out as Eagle came to stand before me.

I spoke before he could open his mouth. "I had to do it."

"Do what?" he said.

"Save that bastard. I triaged you and I knew you'd be okay. He could've died if I didn't help."

"Come here," Eagle said.

I raised an eyebrow at the command in his voice.

He sighed, but it was clear he was at the end of his patience. "Please," he growled with no sign of contrition.

I took the two steps that brought me into his sphere. And then his arms were around me. My head was tucked into that space between his chin and shoulderblades.

"You think I'm mad about that?" His whisper was harsh. His breath brushed the tip of my ear and I shuddered, burrowing deeper into his chest.

"If you're not," I said, "then why are you here?"

"I'm here for you."

I relinquished my spot and leaned back so that I could look into his face. Beside us, Hawk and Owl stood in a semi-circle crowding me in.

Owl shrugged. "I told you; mafia."

"None of you guys are mad that I saved that asshole's life?" I asked.

"I wouldn't have been mad if you left him on the track," Hawk grunted. "But you swore an oath to do no harm."

Nurses didn't swear the Hippocratic Oath, but I didn't bother to correct him.

"We just wanted to make sure you were okay." Hawk leaned past Eagle and kissed me on the cheek.

When Hawk straightened, Owl leaned in on the other side and did the same thing. "I'll see you at home, okay. Pasta will be ready by the time you get there."

I would be invited into their home again? That door wouldn't be shut to me? I watched Hawk and Owl leave through the sliding glass doors. And then I was alone, inside the circle of Eagle's arms, in the middle of a busy emergency room.

I suddenly felt exhausted. I wanted nothing more than to curl up beside Eagle and fall asleep like I had that night I'd slept in his bed. But he wasn't done. He reached in a pocket and brought out a folded document.

"I got you something," he said.

"You got me paperwork?"

"It's the deed. To a house. That I own. You and Toy can stay as long as you like."

"What?"

"And before you say you can't accept it, just remember that I was in an accident with a racist son-of-a-bitch, who nearly took my brother's life, and almost did the same with me, and you saved his life instead of checking on my booboo first. So, you kinda owe me."

I looked at the document. The black ink swam

before my eyes. I looked up at him. His face went out of focus. I must've been really damn tired if I was tearing up. "I'm supposed to say I can't accept this."

"Yeah, I know."

"But I'm too tired."

"Why do you think I'm taking this opportunity to strike now?"

I balled the paper in my fist and returned my head to his chest. "Crow told me I was a distraction for you, like a puzzle."

"He's right. You are a puzzle."

"What happens when you figure me out?"

"I had you figured out the day I met you," Eagle said. "I like making you come apart and then putting you back together. You take care of everybody, Cleo. Somebody needs to take care of you for a change. I would like to be at your service."

His forearms pressed my body into his. For the first time in my life, I didn't want someone to break for me. I forced myself to bend.

"Okay," I whispered.

I felt his lips form a smile as they rested at the cone of my ear.

"But how am I gonna get Toy out of that house?" I asked.

"I have an idea."

TWENTY-FIVE

Toy was trembling in my arms, but at the same time her limbs were limp. It was as though she were a withering leaf that had gone brown and was now falling to the ground on a breeze.

"I can't," she whimpered. "I can't. I can't."

"Count your primes, baby girl."

She took deep, heaving breaths. Not a single digit escaped her lips. Only sobs.

The men of the Watchers Crew along with their girlfriends had come over this morning and packed up the house. Toy had cowered in her room the entire time. Having so much to do in managing the packing and moving, I'd let her. But now the house was empty, the furniture and all our personal effects had been moved across town. All that was left to be moved was Toy.

She slumped on the floor in the foyer. Her entire body from her head to her hands to her knees shook. She was dead weight on the floor.

I looked up at Eagle, my expression helpless. "We can't force her. It will fuck her up for days."

He knelt down in front of her. "Victoria."

She didn't respond.

"I want to play a game with you."

"I can't," she whimpered. "Can't. Can't."

"You don't have to do anything," he said. "Just let Mistress and I take care of you."

He pulled out a velvet bag. From inside the bag, he brought forth a blindfold. He held it in front of Toy. She eyed it, but didn't say anything.

Eagle advanced on her, slowly, as though she were a frightened animal. She was a frightened, injured animal. My heart was breaking as I watched him tie the bindings behind her head.

She didn't protest. As she lost her sight, her hands stopped shaking.

Next, Eagle pulled out earplugs. He placed them in her hand and explained their function. Then, once again, he advanced on her slowly. Toy made no move to resist him. Once both of her ears were plugged her knees stopped knocking.

He scooped her into his arms and she immediately went tense again. He didn't move a step forward or backward. He held still and motioned me over. "Can you put your hands down her pants?"

Toy was wearing loose gym shorts, so it was no great feat. I pushed her panties to the side and found her folds. Within a few strokes they became slippery and she opened for me.

"Walk with me," said Eagle.

As we made our way outside with our cargo, Toy writhed in his arms. But her movements were from familiar manipulations and not from the outdoors. When we climbed in the backseat of my car, she stiffened. Luckily, I knew her body better than she did. I circled her clit with featherlight touches that had her hips reaching for my elusive fingertips.

Owl was in the driver's seat. He started up the engine and took off down the street. He completely ignored the speed limit and my normally sluggish car obeyed his command.

Between Eagle's hands on her breasts and tracing her lips, and my fingers on her clit and stealing into her hungry channel, we kept Toy occupied until we werc in the driveway of our new home.

Our new home happened to be across the street from the Watchers' house. Eagle had told me that they'd been thinking of purchasing the house next door since it went on the market a couple of months ago. He'd closed last week. This afternoon he moved me and Toy in.

With Toy writhing in his arms, he climbed the stairs to her new bedroom. Ellie, Kira, and MK had arranged the room exactly like it had been in our old house. Eagle sat Toy on her bed that had been made with her comforter. He pulled out the earplugs and took off the blindfold. Toy looked around, wide-eyed.

"Where am I?" she asked.

"You're home," he said.

She looked around the room. Her eyes were drooping with exhaustion from the countless orgasms we'd pulled out of her on the car ride. She didn't shake or whimper. She didn't stand up and explore. Instead, she flopped back on the bed and was out like a light.

I turned to Eagle with a grin. "Well, that worked."

He chuckled as he went over and slid Toy's lower half beneath her comforter. Then he turned back to me. "Come on. I'll take you to your room."

My room was largely unpacked. Boxes were lined up against a wall. I had not an ounce of energy to devote to unpacking. Instead, I eyed the large poster bed at the center of the room.

"That's not my bed," I said.

"No." Eagle came up behind me. "It's mine."

I turned and looked up at him. His gaze was unguarded. He stood before me, completely open and vulnerable. The exhaustion from moving house, and transporting Toy, and any other worry I'd had over the past week took a step back. I needed this man on his knees right now. But I was the one who wound up sinking down onto the bed.

Eagle came to kneel over me. He paused, looking down at me. Everywhere his gaze swept burned into my skin. When I realized he was waiting for me, waiting for my permission, I reached up and yanked him down to me.

I hadn't kissed a man in a long time, not in many years. For all my experience with the naughtiest realms of sex, this kiss made me feel like an untried virgin. For all my knowledge of how to make men break, my body went pliant beneath Eagle's.

He didn't take advantage. He didn't try to take control. He followed my lead. My lead was one of slow hunger, of eager fullness, of alert exhaustion.

I wanted this man even as my body was weary. Somehow we became naked. From the corner of my eye I saw the bright neon of a condom as it disappeared between our bodies. And then he was inside me.

We moved in an unhurried, leisurely pace. Our bodies fitting together like long lost puzzle pieces. Our breaths chased after one another and exchanging places in the air as we rose towards a shared climax. I felt him trying to wait for me to go first, but his body had different ideas. We came together in a shuddering, consuming, damn near painful release.

It wasn't until we had both spent ourselves that I realized it; that wasn't fucking. I didn't dare name the thing that it was. Instead, I allowed myself to be wrapped up inside the cocoon of him. Before we fell asleep, he twined his fingers with mine, placed our hands over my heart, and we both fell into a contented sleep in our bed.

SMART BAZTARD -A FREE STORY!

Want more?

*The world of the Watchers Crew isn't over!
When Eagle's brother Prince swaggered onto the page
riding his motorcycle, a whole new world opened up
for me. I wrote the forbidden romance between Prince
and Gabby (Hawk's baby sister).*

*Want to read it?
It's free for members of my reader group!*

Sign up to receive your free copy!
CLICK TO JOIN.

Keep reading for a sneak peek...

Chapter One

Prince's eyes glazed over the string of dental floss that most of the girls wore. Their swimwear was a sea of solid colors that had already been solved by many hands. Bored with the flesh on display, he looked down at the cube in his hands.

Prince had solved his first Rubik's Cube at eight-years-old. At that young age, he'd known intuitively that if he repeated certain patterns, he could solve each color, side by side. Twenty years later, his fingers worked the cube until he'd made a cross-pattern with the yellow blocks. Then he executed a sequence of turns to make L-shapes with those same blocks. A few more twists and turns and he'd have a solid yellow side. The simple algorithm was so ingrained in his mind that his fingers solved the problem without the aid of his eyes, allowing his gaze to once again take in the party around his next door neighbor's pool.

His gaze fixed on a tasteful 1950's style bikini that fully cupped a pair of generous breasts and completely covered a heart-shaped ass. It was the complex color pattern that caught his attention. A

Rubik's Cube had six faces. A bikini had three; four if you counted the back.

Fuck! He was looking at her ass. Prince turned back to the array of dental floss.

He could look at any ass, except hers. But the pattern on her bikini bottom stuck in his mind and he snuck another glance. On the fabric were blocks of the colors; white, red, green, blue, orange, and yellow — just like a Rubik's Cube. The yellow blocks would make a cross-pattern if she just turned to the right. Two twists to the left and the necessary L-shape would form. He worked out the pattern at the apex of her thighs. He knew the exact sequence to solve the triangular pattern on her left breast. He only needed to reverse it on the right breast.

When his gaze met round, pink lips that revealed pearly white teeth, he was stumped. He'd come to the end of the algorithm. He knew that returning Gabby's smile would be a miscalculation, so he looked away.

"Fuck, if I don't love the smell of coeds in the spring." Prince's best friend, Chief, leaned back in the lawn chair and surveyed the field around the pool. His plaid shirt was open revealing copper-toned chest hair that matched the purposefully shaggy red mop on his head and the sculpted ginger mass on his chin. His legs were spread as his light eyes looked over his domain like the Highlanders of his ancestry.

"Coed is another word for jail bait," said Sully. The other man tilted back a light brown beer bottle and then leaned forward in his chair. But his dark eyes locked on the shapely legs of a scantily clad brunette like she was an icicle in the desert sands of his homeland.

Prince's eyes found Gabby again. His attention always came back to her, a pattern from his youth. Five minutes of quiet and he'd have to look up to see what mischief the little girl next door was getting into. If he heard a light trickle of giggling followed by an indignant screech, he would know that his date had found gum in her hair, or a bug in her salad; all the handiwork of little Gabrielleia Hernandez, upset that Prince gave anyone but her his attention.

But those childish games were a thing of the past. Gabby was no longer an adolescent. She was a grown woman. He was too old to play with her like they used to and she was far too young to be anything but jailbait.

"College-fresh women are completely and wholly legal," said Chief. "Tell him, counselor."

Chief directed the comment at Prince. Prince

twisted the cube in his hand and pulled on his legal training. "Technically, the federal age of consent is twelve."

Sully choked on his beer.

Chief dry heaved. "What the fuck, Prince? I said prove me right, not make my balls shrink."

"Once someone reaches eighteen," Prince continued, "they can consensually have sex with another person who is at least eighteen and neither party can be prosecuted for said sexual activities."

Prince's eyes went again to that nineteen-year-old pert ass. A man's hand was on Gabby's ass, passing to the right instead of the left. Prince felt the corners of the Rubik's cube dig into his palms. He'd been working the red face of the puzzle. That color bloomed in his mind as he stared at the hand on the ass, wanting to twist it until it popped out of its socket and off his property.

The *word mine* sounded in his head. Prince clenched his fists. He shook his head. He took a deep breath in, then relaxed his fingers. But the thought wouldn't budge.

Gabby had been his. Or rather, he'd been hers. She'd claimed him when she was just five years old, telling anyone who would listen that she was going to marry Prince when she grew up.

It was cute when she was five and he was fifteen. But when she turned sixteen and began to develop a C cup and she still proclaimed that they would one day be married, it was no longer cute. It was no longer proper. Neither was it proper that he was noticing things about the little girl who'd once been his shadow. And so he'd started making himself sparse, until finally she took the hint and moved on.

Gabby stepped away from the hand of the skinny excuse of a man she called her boyfriend. She turned and raised a perfectly arched eyebrow at him; a clear sign that she had little attention to give to him. She walked away, but the boy gave chase. It was clear that Gabby was done with him. And he wasn't happy about it.

Prince tensed. But he held his seat. He knew that Gabby could handle herself. She'd grown up the only girl on the block with a group of older males watching her every move. Her brother, Hawk, lounged in a chair on one side of the pool with Prince's brother, Eagle. Even if Gabby couldn't handle the skinny prick, those two would be on hand in a split second.

"Like I said," Chief was saying, "freshmen girls are legal. See, bruh, you have plenty of opportunities to put that law degree to use here at home."

"I'm heading down to Washington, D.C. for the interview with the bureau next week," said Prince.

Chief rolled his eyes. "This fucking shit again."

Any talk of Prince's plan to work with the Federal Bureau of Investigation made his smooth-talking friend clam up. Since their youth, Prince, Chief, and Sully had been united in their vigilantism against bullies and injustices. Standing up to schoolyard bullies, chasing drug dealers away from the community center, and challenging racists and bigots out in the street.

But they were all grown men now. It was past time for them to put down their capes, or motorcycle jackets, and get real jobs. That's why Prince was considering this job with the FBI, working for the Civil Rights Division in the Hate Crimes Unit.

"Both of you are selling out," said Chief.

Sully ignored Chief, like normal. The man had always been cool as a cucumber. He didn't work for the Department of Justice, but his allegiance was pledged to the United States. He was in the Army and he was soon headed off for a second tour in the Middle East.

"It's not selling out," said Prince. "We're still all about justice. It's just we do it legally and not like some cartoon comic book superheroes."

"No superhero wears a fucking badge," retorted Chief.

Chief shed his leather jacket. Prince watched as the Baztards Motorcycle Club emblem folded into a neat triangle, just like Prince had designed it to.

"Whatever," Chief said eyeing the fresh meat around the Hernandez's pool. "I'm about to show these little minnows how the big fish do it."

"If you make any of my friends cry, you'll have me to deal with."

Chief's proprietary grin turned into a pained wince. He turned and met with the arched eyebrow of Gabrielleia Hernandez. Gabby was a couple of inches over five foot. The top of her head met Chief's chest, and she had to tilt her head back to glare up at him. But the way Chief's head hung, it was as though a kitten brought down a lion.

"Aw, Gabs," said Chief. "You know I'm just talking shi-" He cleared his throat. "You know I'm just messing around."

"Hmmm," she nodded, then came close to his ear. "You see the blonde in the yellow bikini?" Gabby cocked her head towards the pool. "She's been talking behind my back all year long and then smiling to my face. Go get her."

Chief chuckled, gave Gabby a peck on the

cheek, and then took his marching orders to go get that two-faced blonde. Poor girl. No one crossed Gabby without consequences.

Gabby watched Chief approach her frenemy with a wicked grin. Then she turned back to Prince and Sully. Prince held his breath, but she didn't turn to him.

"You doing all right, Sully?" she asked. "Can I get you another beer?"

"Thanks, Gabby, but I'm about to call it a night." Sully rose and pulled on his club jacket. The night was warm, but he'd rode his bike and the leather would protect him from the elements.

"Hawk says you're headed back overseas soon?"

"Yeah, second tour. Afghanistan, this time."

Gabby winced, pressing her lips together in a slight grimace, but quickly turned her frown upside down. "Can I write to you? I don't want you to get behind on *The Real Housewives*."

"Can't walk around Kabul not knowing if Bethany and Jill ever make up," Sully said with a grave face that made Gabby giggle.

He bent down and gave Gabby a kiss on top of her head. She put her arms around him for a hug. Sully startled. He wasn't so good with affection and Gabby always doled it out in spades. When she released him, he nodded to Prince and then headed out of the Hernandez's backyard. That left Prince alone with Gabby.

Prince hated the awkwardness between the two of them. It had never been that way before. Gabby had been attached to his hip before she could crawl. She'd been his shadow since she could walk. She'd struggled to keep up behind him when she could run. But then her increasing breast size came between them. Her widening hips made him take a step back. Her lush lips, whose pout he used to find adorable, had his eyes glued to the floor. But looking down he saw the pink polish on her toes and it made his pants feel uncomfortable.

"Hey," she said. Her voice had been high pitched for most of her life. Now it was husky and sex-ladened. "I made these for you."

Gabby produced a small plate of sandwiches. Charcoal chicken with a homemade, creamy chipotle sauce. Prince groaned and grabbed for the sandwiches. He took a bite. It was delicious as always. Gabby was an amazing cook. He'd devoured the first one before he remembered his manners.

"Thanks, Gabs."

She grinned, and just like that he saw his Gabby. But it was strange that she didn't come any closer to him for a hug. She was always hanging on him, snuggling up under him. Not anymore and he was sorry for it.

"So, how was your first semester at college?" he asked.

Gabby shrugged. "They didn't kick me out."

Academics had never been Gabby's strong suit. Social situations, cooking, and music were.

"How's orchestra going?" he asked and then finished off the second sandwich.

"I made first chair last month," she grinned.

"That's my girl." He reached up his hand, and she slapped it with all five of her fingers. Unfortunately, it was the hand he'd used to shovel food in his mouth and he got some of the chipotle sauce on her palm.

Gabby giggled and reached for a beach towel. She wiped her fingers, and then his.

"I hope you'll come to the end-of-year concert," she said as she dropped the towel back onto one of the lounge chairs.

Prince didn't miss the hope in her voice. He also didn't miss that she held onto his now cleaned fingers. He had been a constant fixture at her concerts since she picked up the cello. He'd never missed a recital or concert.

"Sorry, Gabs." He rubbed his thumb over hers just like he'd done when she was a little girl. The move often settled her when she was upset. "I may not make this one."

Gabby lowered her lashes and pressed her lips into a tight pout. Prince had to look away. He could not resist the pout.

"I might be out of town." He might as well get this over with. "I got offered that job with the Bureau."

Her eyes widened, and the pout fell away, replaced by open-mouthed astonishment. "In D.C.?"

Prince had the urge to fold her into his arms like when she was a toddler. To kiss the booboo. To rock her to sleep. But he didn't have a chance to do any of those things.

"Gabby, can I talk to you?"

Both Gabby and Prince turned to her boyfriend. Their hands were still entwined. Prince had forgotten. For a long time, it had been so natural to hold her hand. That word sounded again in his mind; *mine.* But he knew that wasn't right. She could never be anything more than the little girl he used to hold, the girl next door that he used to watch over, the teen he'd watch out for. Slowly, he unfurled his fingers from the young woman's and he let her go.

"I'm going to take off," Prince said.

He didn't look back as he walked away. He wasn't ready to go home, and so he headed for the pool house. Before he went in, he chanced a look back.

Prince watched as Gabby put her hands on her hips and squared off with the boyfriend. He remembered when those hips were straight lines. They were all curves now. When she put her hands on her square hips as a little girl, there was no way anyone would win an argument against her. Now, with all those curves, well, there still was no way anyone was winning an argument against her. Gabby had always been able to bend the men in her life to her will, and this skinny prick would be no different.

Prince watched as the skinny prick's head drooped. Gabby raised a hand with her finger pointing to the gate. After the prick shuffled off, she turned back to her guests. She plastered on a smile that would make her mother proud and continued to play hostess.

Prince grinned. Nothing could shirk his girl. He shook his head. She wasn't his girl anymore. She never would be his girl. Which was why Prince needed to get out of here and take that job in D.C.

CHAPTER Two

Gabby waved to the last of her friends. The pool party had been a success, but she felt like a failure. She was struggling in school, but that wasn't new. She'd spent a good deal of the evening fighting with Charlie, again, more old news. At least now she was free of him and his nagging. She'd heard her brother and Eagle complain about women constantly calling and hanging on them, seeking their attention, and tracking their movements. She felt a weight lifted off her now that her boyfriend was kicked to the curb.

Having a boyfriend hadn't been at all what she expected. Charlie hadn't had a lot of interesting things to say. He hadn't wanted to play board games like she used to do with Prince. He was a vegetarian, for god's sake, and picked at most of the food she'd made him. All he wanted to do was get his hand up her skirts and down her panties. Or bathing suit.

Well, he could take his non-interesting, vegetable grubbing, nagging self onto the next girl, because she was done.

"Gabs?"

Gabby looked up at her best friend, Diniece, who stood in the gate between the backyard and the street. Diniece had pulled a pair of jeans over her long brown legs and swept her intricate braids up into a ponytail.

The two girls had met during Freshman Orientation and had been inseparable ever since. Diniece had been instrumental in getting Gabby to go out and explore the social side of being a college student. And for a time, Gabby had actually managed to push aside her deep-seated feelings for the guy next door. But the moment she saw Prince tonight, all of those feelings came back.

Gabby had seen Prince looking at her in her colorful swimsuit. She'd chosen it because the colors reminded her of a Rubik's Cube, Prince's favorite game. His gaze had been locked on her ass as though he was trying to figure out how to solve the puzzle of her. And when he'd held her hand, she'd felt the same electricity she'd always felt between the two of them.

"I'm gonna head out with Cheryl and Walt," Diniece was saying. "You coming?"

Gabby had seen Prince go off into the pool house and she hadn't seen him leave. The last thing she wanted to do was go out and feign interest in frat boys. "I'm gonna stay here and clean up a bit. But you go on ahead."

Diniece cocked her head to the side and regarded her friend. "I can stay behind and do the ice cream after a break up thing with you."

"No need," Gabby sighed. "Charlie wasn't worthy of a tub of ice cream."

"Okay, girl." Diniece brought Gabby in for a hug. "Shopping therapy tomorrow?"

"Definitely."

Gabby watched her friend walk out the gate and then she turned to the pool house. Technically, it was the Hernandez's pool. But with Eagle and Hawk being best friends and Gabby constantly clinging to Prince as a child, and not to mention their mom and her dad working closely together, the families both claimed it.

Gabby opened the door to see a large man sprawled out on the couch. Prince had a beer in one hand and the remote in the other. He looked up to see her close the door. His unfocused eyes went wary, and then shifted to concern.

"Hey, monkey?" He sat his beer and the remote down and stood. "What's the matter?"

The nickname had come about when she was three and would wrap all of her limbs around him in an effort to escape bedtime, or nap time, or going to daycare, or for any reason that she could think up to stay with Prince.

Gabby was the first to admit that she could be manipulative. She had to be when she was surrounded by three large males who could best her with their pinky fingers. She learned to bat her eyelashes, pout her lips, and play on the protective instincts of her brother, Eagle, and Prince.

"Was it that prick?" Prince came to stand before her. "Where is he? What did he do?"

Gabby shook her head, batting her eyelashes. "He's gone. It's over between us."

"Yeah, I thought so." Prince scanned her body as though looking for any evidence of wounds. Finding none, he looked into her eyes. "What happened?"

"Last night, Charles wanted me to do something that I didn't want to do."

Prince's nostrils flared like a lion ready to strike. It made Gabby feel tingles in her belly.

"Don't go ballistic," she said. "I thought I wanted to do it. But when he did it, I decided I didn't like it. He got mad that I wouldn't let him try again. So, I broke up with him."

Prince bared his teeth when he spoke. "What did he try to do?"

Gabby tugged her lower lip in her mouth before

she responded. She felt her cheeks flush as she said the words. But she was unsure if she was embarrassed by what Charlie had done or if she felt excited talking sex with Prince.

"He finger popped me," she said.

"Finger popped?" Prince whispered the words. His brown skin looked like it was turning green.

"He stuck his thumb into my vagina." She knew she didn't need to clarify, but her words worked.

Prince's protective instincts kicked in. He looked ready to murder poor Charlie. Gabby knew she just needed to turn that mindless aggression to a better cause.

"I don't understand how that was supposed to feel good?" She crossed her arms over her chest and gave herself a squeeze. "I didn't like it. His hands were rough and it hurt. I mean, it's not like I was ready for sex. But I was willing to take a step. Now, I don't know if I'm interested."

"He didn't know what he was doing."

"I figured," she said taking a step into Prince. "I mean *you* have rough hands." She trailed a finger down his forearm to the fleshy part of his thumb. "Whenever you touch me it never hurts."

He took a step back, but her hands snaked around his hips and locked at his low back. She unloaded the rest of her arsenal, looking up at him from under long lashes, and then there was the pout. She knew Prince could never resist the pout.

"Gabby..." Prince warned, his tone no-nonsense.

But she had one more card to play. And this one never failed. She tilted her head and changed tactics.

"It's just that... You've always been my best tutor. And it's been so hard not having your help to navigate college. And now there are all these intimate situations."

She tightened her hold on him. He didn't retreat. Her body was pressed flush against his. She could feel his heavy breaths that began in his belly, rose to his chest, and landed on her forehead. He wasn't holding her, but she had him.

"I just want to know what it's supposed to feel like," she said. "You know, for when the next boyfriend goes down there."

Prince's body tensed, and he cursed under his breath.

"Please," she said again. "Show me what's supposed to happen. I trust you more than anyone."

She felt his breaths rise and fall a little faster. She felt the rumble in his belly as it pressed into hers. Something firm pressed into her belly as well.

Prince's hand slipped a little lower on her waist.

She watched the calculations play out in his hazel eyes. She'd never been this close to her goal, and she wasn't going to let this opportunity pass her by.

Gabby knew that she and Prince were meant to be. It was one of her first memories. She'd never understood why they had to wait until an arbitrary number of years to pass for them to be together. But she was of age now. There was nothing stopping them, except his hesitation.

"He pinched me down there. Was that supposed to feel good?"

"No," Prince growled with disgust. "When a man touches a woman... there." He swallowed, but he didn't back away from her. "It's a sensitive area. You have to treat it with care."

"So you would rub me softly, with the pad of your finger?"

"Yeah," he breathed. "Softly."

"Which finger?" she asked. "Your thumb? Your index finger? Your middle finger? Is there a difference?"

His eyes were foggy as they gazed at her. The fingers of his right hand trembled as they rested on her hip, like they were fighting to hold still. "With my index finger. You have most control over its dexterity."

"Because you use it to write with? That makes sense."

"Yeah." He swallowed and then gulped down another breath of air.

"Would you make circles?" she asked. "Or a windshield wiping motion? Or something else?"

"I..." He had to swallow again. His thumb was on the waistband of her bikini bottom. It made little circles just below her belly button.

"Prince?"

"Yeah, Gabs?"

"I feel achy down there. Like I'm hot and swollen. That didn't happen before. Is that normal?"

"Yeah, monkey." His thumb slipped inside the waist band and rubbed circles in her tight curls. "That's perfectly normal."

Gabby felt it was safe to unlock her arms from his waist. With one hand she slipped one side of her bikini bottoms down and then the other until the garment hit the floor. "So there's nothing wrong with me?"

"No, sweetheart," he sighed as he looked down at her bare torso. "You're perfect."

Prince's thumb burrowed through her damp curls and found the hood of her bud. Gabby's knees buckled at the impact of his rough finger pad. Prince caught her with his free arm.

"I feel like I need to lay down," she said.

Prince scooped her up in his arms and carried her over to the couch. The moment her butt made impact with the cushion, Gabby spread her legs. Prince let out a choked sound as he hovered over her, staring down at her bare sex.

"What happens next?" she asked, running her bare toes along the cushion. She could feel his hot breaths cool her sex as he panted above her.

Prince lifted his gaze to focus on her. His eyes cleared. Gabby froze for a moment. Had she made a miscalculation?

"You need to learn how to do this for yourself," he said finally.

Gabby breathed an internal sigh of relief. "Show me."

Prince swallowed. He took a deep breath and let it out, and then he reached for her. With one hand on each thigh, he opened her legs wider. His gaze was cool and assessing.

"This is your clitoris. Your bud is average size so you don't need a firm touch. Just light circles in a clockwise motion-"

"Like this?" Gabby reached down and swirled

her index finger around her swollen bud. It didn't feel as good as when Prince had briefly touched it with the pad of his large thumb. But having his eyes on her was bringing her to her climax quicker than when she touched herself in the dark of her dorm room with him in her mind.

"Good girl," whispered Prince. "Just like that." He pressed her thighs open wider, stretching her labia apart, pulling at the hood surrounding her bud.

His hot exhale against her swollen bud made her belly tighten. His slow inhale while his gaze fixed on the juices running down her legs made her core clench.

"Prince..." she moaned.

"Keep circling, monkey. Let it happen."

And so she did. She let the waves of sensation build inside her. She let that spring that resided in the center of her belly coil around until her toes began to curl and her breathing shallowed.

"A little faster. That's a good girl."

Her hips were now lifting off the cushion as she made passes over her bud. She wanted to press her legs together to help relieve some of the tension, but Prince's grip on her was absolute.

"Slow down, monkey."

"I don't want to."

"Trust me."

Gabby was used to having her own way. Prince was one of the people who typically gave it to her. But the soft plea in his voice had her fingers slowing down their motion. And the effect of the halted progress shattered her.

Slowing down her touch made the orgasm come at her even faster. But as it came for her, it built up steam, like a snowball rolling down a mountain. It picked up other snow, packing it on until it was a boulder that came rushing down the north face.

The orgasm knocked her back. Her hips arched off the couch. Her back bowed. Her heels dug into the couch cushions. A desperate gasp escaped her lungs. She had to shut her eyes to try to contain some sense of herself. Behind her eyelids, she saw stars and colors collide, reform, and then burst.

When she opened her eyes, she saw Prince. He was staring at her with a look in his eyes she'd never seen before. Was this it? Was he finally coming to understand that they were meant to be? Was he finally realizing that he loved her?

Not in the way that he'd loved her as a child. Not the adoration he showed her as a little girl. Was he finally seeing her as the woman that she was, the woman who was meant for him?

Gabby raised her hand to his cheek. His upper body shook on its impact. He inhaled and his eyes grew larger. He turned his face to her fingers. He swallowed once, twice. Then he opened his mouth and attacked her index finger.

He pulled it into his mouth and sucked. His eyes closed and he sucked her finger. A groan sounded deep inside and still he continued to suck. He let go of her finger with a long lick.

Then his head slowly turned back to her, back to the core of her. He took one breath, and then he was on her.

His mouth latched on to her entire core. His tongue worked in circles, figure eights, and a back and forth motion that had Gabby trembling.

He let go, coming up for air, and her hips followed him. He dipped his head and lapped up the juices that had spilled down her thighs. He suckled first the right and then the left labia. He stuck his tongue deep inside her virgin hole, swirling and burrowing until another orgasm made its way up the hill. It picked up speed and then crashed into her so hard that she wrapped her thighs around Prince's head.

Prince patiently unfolded her thighs' grip from his head. All the while not breaking the hold his mouth had on her. He moved his attentions up to her clitoris. He made that same pattern of circles, eights, and swipes at her bud. He sucked on her until Gabby was a writhing mess and a third orgasm rolled through her body.

The third one shook her so hard her eyes teared. She closed her legs, placing a protective hand at the apex of her thighs. She curled into a fetal position as the pleasure continued to assault her in aftershocks.

"Fuck," she heard Prince whisper. "Fuck."

Yes, she thought. That's exactly what she wanted. For her Prince to fuck her. She rolled over onto her back and gazed up at the man of her dreams, the man she knew she was born to spend the rest of her life with. She smiled up at him, intoxicated by his touch, under the influence of his tongue, and punch drunk with pleasure.

But Prince was not grinning. He wasn't even smiling. His hands were in his tightly curled hair. His eyes were filled with horror. His mouth was set in a grim line.

"What did I just do?" His voice was hoarse, and the words were forced.

Gabby blinked, trying to make her mind understand what could possibly be the matter. But her limbs still weren't working properly. She couldn't hold herself up, much less sit up.

"I don't know what came over me," he said as he backed away from her. His movements staggering and uncoordinated, like he was drunk as well.

Gabby opened her mouth, but her throat was raw from all the moaning. She couldn't form words to stop his hasty retreat. She couldn't reach out to grab him as he backed away from her.

"I'm so sorry, Gabby. That will never happen again."

He turned out the door and was gone.

Of course that's not the end.
It's only the beginning.

The battle of wills and desire between these two is epic. Want to read the whole story?

Sign up for Ines Johnson's newsletter and it's yours!
CLICK TO JOIN!